KILL ME NOW

ALSO BY TIMMY REED

Tell God I Don't Exist
The Ghosts That Surrounded Them
Stray/Pest
Miraculous Fauna
Star Backwards
IRL

KILL ME NOW

A Novel

TIMMY REED

COUNTERPOINT
BERKELEY, CALIFORNIA

KILL ME NOW

This book is a work of fiction. Names, characters, places, and incidents are the product of the author's imagination or are used fictitiously. Any resemblance to actual events is unintended and entirely coincidental.

Library of Congress Cataloging-in-Publication Data
Names: Reed, Timmy, author.
Title: Kill me now : a novel / Timmy Reed.
Description: Berkeley, CA : Counterpoint Press, [2017]
Identifiers: LCCN 2017030650 | ISBN 9781619025370 (hardcover)
Subjects: LCSH: Teenage boys—Fiction. | GSAFD: Bildungsromans.
Classification: LCC PS3618.E43587 K55 2018 | DDC 813/.6—dc23
LC record available at https://lccn.loc.gov/2017030650

Jacket designed by Debbie Berne
Book interior by Wah-Ming Chang

COUNTERPOINT
2560 Ninth Street, Suite 318
Berkeley, CA 94710
www.counterpointpress.com

Printed in the United States of America
Distributed by Publishers Group West

10 9 8 7 6 5 4 3 2 1

To Baltimore and adolescence: Best wishes.

Love,
Timmy

It is easier to build strong children than to repair broken men.

—FREDERICK DOUGLASS

KILL ME NOW

~

One time I tried keeping track of the things that happened to me in a journal. I figured that I'm gonna be OLD and DEAD one day and the only way of making sure that anything would get remembered by me or anyone else was if I wrote it down and since nobody else could do it for me I took on the job myself. I charged a composition book on my parents' account at the school store. It had black and white speckles on the cover. It looked like TV static. I wrote my name inside.

The first few entries were daily. I would write the date at the top of every one. That sort of detail felt important. Sometimes the entries were short and sometimes they kind of like rambled, but they were never very good. The journal was boring because nothing exciting ever seemed to happen and I usually forgot to write about it afterward when it did. Or I'd try to write it out as accurately as I could but it'd just end up seeming dull and even sort of made-up when I went to reread it. So I stopped writing in the book every day. Instead of listing all the dumb little events that happened, I tried to write about my FEELINGS when I had them instead. I wouldn't have to be so meticulous or disciplined if I was going to write about FEELINGS, was what I figured. But I had problems with that too, because I didn't actually HAVE that many SPECIFIC feelings to speak of. And whenever I did feel something it was just like what I was talking about earlier. I'd forget the details afterward—whatever made the feeling seem important in the first place—like the way you forget a dream when you go to replay it in the morning.

And a lot of the time I was just too lazy to write in my journal. Whenever I *would* get a feeling down on paper, it'd come off as stupid or shallow or embarrassing to have even had in the first place. Unworthy. And then there were the times when I knew there was stuff I should've put in the journal but when I sat on my bed and tried to write it out, I couldn't do it. I was scared or something. Even though I knew nobody else was going to read it. And even then I doubt they could decipher my handwriting. One thing about me is that I was never what you call particularly courageous. And my script is fucking awful.

Anyway the journal sucked and after a while I ended up tossing it out with the trash. The notebook was mostly empty anyhow. I was probably nine or ten years old at the time. Now the whole thing seems pretty fucking stupid. But then again, here I am writing this stuff down in a composition book just like when I was a little kid so I guess I'll let you figure out who and what stupid is for yourself. I let most people call me "Retard" for instance, although my real name is Miles Lover.

~

I don't know how people started calling me "Retard." A lot of people get called that I'm sure. I say it all the time for instance. But for some reason with me the name stuck and even managed to take on the status of a proper noun. Maybe it was my handwriting. Maybe not. When I was little I thought it was on account of the purple birthmark that covers my right eye like a bruise. My mother calls it a "winespot." Having a winespot doesn't mean I'm actually retarded or anything like that, but I used to be pretty fucking sensitive about it. So I guess I just assumed it had something to do with my nickname. Now that I'm older and not such a pussy about it, I realize it's probably something else. It might be I'm called "Retard" because of the way it fits in front of my last name, but I doubt it. There are other things that would fit better, make more sense, like Dick . . . Maybe it's because I talk too loud. People are always making signs at me to lower my voice. And I vomit often. I get dizzy and nauseous. Especially this time of year. Allergies, I think. The pollen is awful. The whole world is yellow-green around the edges. I sneeze. It's everything else too. My fingers bleed because I bite my nails. I'm always spitting on the sidewalk. I draw on my sneakers and the back of my hands when I ought to be listening to people that are smarter than me. I fidget. I chew on my pens until they explode in my mouth and the ink gets stuck in the cracks between my teeth and people laugh. My shoelaces are always coming untied. I sweat in my sleep and wake up very cold. My short-term memory sucks donkey wang. Everything I touch somehow gets lost. People tell me I look confused. I'm always getting in trouble for it, for not listening. I exist in a constant state of reprimand. I squint . . . But fuck all that. I don't know. It's gotta be something else. Something bigger. Something about me. A quality. Something that shouts: RETARD!

Anyway, people are always introducing me to strangers that way. And I don't bother to correct them. I'm too proud.

They must have started calling me "Retard" when I *was* pretty young I think, because I remember hearing it a whole lot when I was a kid . . . I thought I was so damn clever back then. My favorite thing was to be completely literal about stuff, which would really get under people's skin. That's probably why I did it in the first place. For instance, whenever somebody called me "ignorant" I'd explain how "ignorant" means "untaught" and that I was quite well-educated for my age, which was like seven or eight or whatever. Likewise, the first few times anyone called me "retarded" I probably told them the word meant "slow" before running off at top speed, grinning like a lunatic.

So I guess I was pretty retarded as a little kid or whatever, but who isn't? And this thing with being really literal about everything was only a phase thank god. After that I didn't say anything when people called me ignorant or retarded. I embraced it. "Retard" was even sewn on the back of my windbreaker after my rec league lacrosse team won the C division championship in sixth grade. Miles "Retard" Lover. My coach got WAY ANGRY about it though. I felt bad because I figured he probably knew somebody for real retarded. And I had reminded him of a bad situation or whatever. Don't worry, I stopped wearing the jacket after that. I'm not some kind of asshole.

~

My mother harbors a superstition that on the first day of every month when you wake up the first two words you are supposed to say are "RABBIT, RABBIT." It's true. Not the superstition I mean, but that she believes it. Just like that, "RABBIT, RABBIT," twice in a row. If you do this you will have good luck until the end of the month. Then you have to do it all over again for the next month. If you forget to say "RABBIT, RABBIT" when you wake up on the first and you say another two words instead, like "Good morning" or "OJ, please," you will have very bad luck for the rest of the month. Except there is a way around this. To reverse the bad luck you have to walk up and down the stairs ten times backwards, repeating the phrase over and over again as you do it.

My mother claims the origin of this superstition goes way back, but none of my aunts ever remember it when I ask them. I always suspected she made the whole thing up. She must've started passing the superstition on pretty early though, because I've known about it ever since I can remember. I even did it myself for a while. Or tried to at least. I usually forgot missing the first of the month until well into the next one. But I tried. And this was long after I stopped believing in things like Santa Claus. I thought it was fun to walk up and down the steps backwards, I guess.

~

I'm at my father's new place watching a show about reptiles on his big plasma screen—he didn't buy one until he moved out the last time and was living all by himself, the selfish prick—and right now he's in the office either sifting through piles of paperwork or copying music or playing Internet bridge, I'm sure. The show I'm watching is in awesome high definition and the footage is profoundly clear. I don't even need to squint without my glasses, which I refuse to wear ever until I can drive and still maybe not even then. Anyway, the reptiles on the screen look giant and realer than real. The rain falls like bullets all around me out of my father's surround sound. I can feel the jungle. The water, the life. I'm absolutely astounded. I'm also totally stoned off some gross shwag I smoked in the back lot behind my father's rowhome, which is full of crows and high grasses and random bulldozers and cracked mud patches, until this Mexican work crew finishes building all the houses that are supposed to go there.

The narrator of the show is profiling the strangest creature I ever saw, a long snaky kind of lizard with tiny, almost useless legs. He kind of walks, kind of slithers through this thick rainforest all by himself.

An endangered species that lives all alone. I'm fixated by him. He eats a small mousy thing. Apparently only once a year, in the springtime, which is like our fall or whatever, does this animal, which I like to call a "snizard"—him being part snake part lizard—ever seek out another one of its own. And that's only for a single violent fuck in the bush. They bite each other when they do it. I watched. So the snizard's life strikes me as a pretty lonely one. All alone in the jungle. No friends. Nowhere to belong. He can't hang with the snakes for being too much a lizard and vice versa with the lizards for being too much a snake. A snizard fears and is feared alike by his peers. Actually . . . He has no peers. He's a loner. A freak. Born with outcast status. Forced by nature to walk alone. But a snizard can barely walk . . .

I'm even starting to find this thing pretty cute, with its soft round head and pathetic little claws, when I hear my dad moving around in the kitchen. He's probably making a Turkey Spam sandwich, which I personally find disgusting. He eats a lot of these now. He eats them cold with cheese. Gross. Sometimes he offers to make me one. I just say no.

So I'm listening cautiously to his movements on the other side of the wall. I actually hear him fart in there. I cringe when I hear it. I know he's going to come in the living room and sit down. I sort of tense up, which I kind of feel bad about, which makes me even more tense. He comes in and stands over me in his worn-out khakis and his old college sweatshirt, smiling. I can smell the sandwich in his hand. I cover my nose with my sleeve.

"Whatcha watchin', kiddo?" he asks me. He has this big dumb smile on his mug. Like he is about to play with a toddler. Or a Martian. He hasn't sat down yet. He's still standing there.

"Television," I say.

He looks over at the screen. I try not to look at him.

"Anything good?"

"Um, no. Just, um, TV. You know. Television in general."

"Just TV?"

I nod, but don't say anything, eyeballs glued to the screen like I have blinders on.

I know my dad hates channel surfing. He finds it annoying. He would rather just sit and watch a TV show all the way through. Even the commercials! So I bring up the interactive guide and start flipping around like a madman, going back and forth through all this shit I know he's probably too old to enjoy anyway. After a minute he just sort of slides back out of the room in his socks. I can hear him in the hallway, shuffling off to look at the computer. My muscles go all loose with relief.

When I go back to the reptile program to check up on the snizard, the narrator has moved on to something else. It's a giant chameleon-thing with a forked tongue and sharp-looking scales like feathers and a chest that can be puffed out all proud until you can see right through it and tell that it is hollow inside.

~

My father's new rowhome is located in a gated community at the south end of Homeland. My mother's is at the north end of Roland Park, in a similar community. Roland Park and Homeland sit right next to each other at the north end of the city, separated only by four well-funded private schools, two Protestant churches, a gourmet food market, one cathedral, a seminary, a monastery, and a convent full of nuns. No joke. They like god a lot around here.

Both neighborhoods are full of big old worn-in houses with front yards and backyards and families inside. Our old place is located on

Charles Street, in between the two neighborhoods, just up the road from the Cathedral of Mary Our Queen.

The house is pretty big and kind of old. It's crawling with ivy and wisteria. I like the ivy. It makes me feel like the house is alive. The dark green vines have even grown over some of the upstairs windows and what used to be a fish pond in the backyard. The old place has a decent-sized yard too. But inside it's pretty much empty at this point, with random furniture sitting around under sheets of dusty oilcloth.

People are always being led through by our realtor. Our realtor is a family friend. A few years ago, my father used to hook up with her oldest daughter. My mother doesn't blame our realtor for her daughter's indiscretions, although I feel pretty uncomfortable being in the same room with the three of them at one time. Or any of them alone for that matter. But the power is still on in the old house and the pipes still work, so I go back there by myself a lot. Mostly just to get away from people.

My folks are in the middle of a divorce if you can't already tell, and it's been a long time coming. They've been separated three times before and this was the fourth. I'm not sure why they keep getting back together. Their story was always that they stayed together for the sake of the kids and sometimes for each other, but I suspect they did it more for the sake of their joint financial situation. I'm, like, a realist if you know what I mean. I know people are willing to put up with a whole lot of shit in a lifetime just to maintain some stability. And I doubt if their union ever made us kids any happier in the first place. Personally, I would have PREFERRED if they got divorced a long time ago, which is like a lot of my friends' parents' situations. Except that I used to practically WORSHIP my old house. Now I have to face the fact of sooner or later not having it, which is gonna suck.

But anyway my folks live separately now, again, in separate rowhomes in separate developments about a mile away from one another, and I go back and forth between them all the time. I like being at Mom's more I guess because the food is way better, but my father has the sweeter television.

~

I'm a total insomniac, especially during summer. I'm partially nocturnal. I can't help it. Since I'm not old enough to drive yet and a lot of my friends still have curfews, I end up alone a lot real late at night, although sometimes somebody will sleep over or something and then I won't be. Anyway this means I'm usually up doing all kinds of crazy shit when the rest of the world is sleeping. Like a vampire. Or opossum.

Well, not that crazy. But a lot of skateboarding and fireworks and listening to music and smoking weed. And maybe getting a little bit weird too, you know . . . Sometimes things just seem crazier when you're all alone in the middle of the night is all, like everything is charged up with electricity. It's easy to freak yourself out in these situations. It's kind of like being a little kid again. Things are scary. Not that I believe in monsters or anything. Not really. But you can get worked up enough that it sometimes FEELS like crazy shit is happening late at night. So you stay away from certain shadows or little places while you're out walking or skating around. Sometimes it's like you're being watched. Or followed. Like stalked. Not because there's actually anything that you ought to be scared of, you just get freaked out is all. I'd say it was the weed making me paranoid, but I remember things being that way a lot before I ever even tried smoking it.

But for the most part, I just stay up and watch skate videos. I look at magazines. Sometimes I secretly set up my GI Joes in front of this rad homemade wartime panorama, complete with fake blood and exploding landmines drawn in paint pen, with spaghetti intestine and all sorts of body parts flying everywhere, which I made back when I was still into all that stuff but have secretly kept in my closet ever since. If my sisters have any of their friends over, I might wander in and fuck around with them a while to kill time. But the point is, I like to stay up a lot, especially during summer.

~

Secret: When I was just a little guy, I used to be so scared of my dad that I would lie awake at night praying that the Rock would come over and kick his ass. It's not like that anymore. He seems more pathetic now. Not the Rock, my dad. Although the Rock seems sort of sad too.

~

Curfew in Baltimore City is supposedly midnight. It only applies to us kids though. And I've only been brought home for curfew once. They rang my doorbell and woke my parents up. My folks were still living together in our old house at the time. My father tried to be polite I guess, but he was groggy. He just sort of grunted and let me inside. My mother offered to fix the police some coffee. The fuzz said no thank you and split. I went back out like ten minutes later.

I've never been arrested in Baltimore City, but the county has gotten me twice. One time for skateboarding in Towson, on the ledges outside the courthouse. They grabbed me and a few other kids and confiscated our boards until trial. I had to do community service to get mine back. Lining the soccer fields at some lame elementary school. By that time I already had a new board, but they made me do it anyway.

The next time I got popped was also in Towson. I was standing outside the movie theater when a fight broke out between some older goth kid and a boy I used to play rec league lacrosse with. I wasn't on either side of the fight. I was just watching. I usually stick around to watch a fight when it happens. They don't last very long. Anyway, a cruiser rolled up and two young police officers got out. The fight stopped immediately. But for some reason, because I'm stupid I guess, I took off running. If I'd thought about it I would've stayed put. Blended into the crowd. I hadn't done anything wrong. But I never think when I'm supposed to. Instead I take off running. When the pig caught me, he had his gun drawn. Like I was some kind of threat. I'm a pretty small dude, for chrissakes, and I was *running*. Cops are such dickheads. Being in control gives them a hard-on. And they're always looking for someplace to ram it. Anyway, they searched me down and found a half-pint of bourbon that I was going to bring into the movie. Plus a gram of shwag. I had to go to court again. I had the same lawyer as before, he was one of my mother's friends. I ended up getting a P.B.J., but I had to see a case manager once a month and regularly attend Alateen meetings, which is basically the same thing as AA, but for kids.

My probation officer's last name was PAYNE. Seriously. Payne. Think she was trying to make a point? She was a giant for one thing. A giant*ess*. Like eleven-feet-tall. She lived in a cave behind the county jail. The jail itself was air conditioned, but her cave was hot as hell. She had a fan though. It blew a gentle whisper through the office, which tickled her diplomas up off the wall like water through the gills of a shark. The whole place smelled like a pine forest. Because of this,

I suspected her of spiking her coffee with gin. She slurped it from a human skull that had once belonged to her predecessor. At least that's what I imagined. She enjoyed collecting other things as well. Coins, stamps, memorial koozies, framed needlepoint mottos, and rubber plastic trolls. She hoarded them like a dragon. The trolls were static-haired and naked, missing their genitals. You know the ones. They watched me with googly eyes as I gave urine specimens behind her file cabinet, which I always guessed was full of stolen comic books. Miss Payne had tremendous calf muscles, I remember, coated with either leg hairs or parasites. I couldn't be sure. I can never be sure about anything . . .

Alateen wasn't as bad as all that. There were even a few hot girls in my group. One of them was a cokehead. I had the biggest crush on her. But then she stopped going to meetings. They had the Twelve Steps and what's called the Big Book, but I didn't pay much attention to either of those, although I did enjoy some of the stories people were telling. One kid was like seventeen and he knew about a million beer-drinking games. He was always talking about it. He seemed very competitive. Another girl was this desperate fat-ass who couldn't stop stealing her grandmother's booze. I felt bad for her. One time I thought she was going to cry during her testimony. I wanted to give her a hug. But I didn't. I spent most of my time at those meetings engaged in what they call "cross-talk." That means speaking without raising your hand. I didn't do it on purpose. I just always forgot to raise my hand. At the end of each meeting we formed a circle and held hands to pray the Serenity Prayer. That's where you ask god for the serenity to accept the things you cannot change and the courage to change the things you can. Eventually I got off my probation and then I immediately stopped attending those meetings. So I guess the prayer worked. At least for me it did.

~

Since my parents moved into their respective places, I've gotten to know some of my new neighbors a little bit. The kind of people that live in both communities are mostly the same. Divorced people, old people, and families. At South Homeland Mews where my father lives, they have a pool, a sauna, weight machines, and a treadmill and stuff. The houses are slightly smaller than in my mother's community. There are a decent amount of thirty-something professional-type people living there and some gay couples too. Probably because of the pool and workout space. But otherwise the developments are basically the same, I guess.

Like I said, the rowhomes are a little bigger at Roland Park Northway, which is maybe why there are more kids, but they're mostly all younger than me. In fact I think I might be the oldest. One kid is this geek who just moved up from DC. Our mothers met and became friends. His name is Donald Diamond and his mother's name is Sandy. Sandy is hot. She goes jogging all the time in a leotard and I just want to kick her son's ass so fucking bad.

Donald has these big round lips like a girl. I always feel like punching him. He's one of those asshole kids who pretends that they have never masturbated before and shit like that. He's probably not allowed to watch R-rated movies or eat sugar. I hate him.

The other day, Donald comes over. We're playing video games. He keeps beating me one-on-one in NHL hockey, which is fine except I was already playing a season against the computer when he came in and I didn't invite this kid over anyway. I don't want him to start thinking he can just drop by all the time uninvited.

Laughing, he asks me if it's true that I used to let all the kids at my old school, which he now goes to, call me "Retard" when I went there. I don't know why this should bother me because it's true, I do let everyone call me that and I even call myself that sometimes, like when I had that jacket made up. But bother me it does when this little pussy asks me about it, laughing all the while like it's FUNNY I let people call me "Retard." Which I guess it probably is to some people. But at the moment I don't see why it should be funny to him.

Instead of punch his face, which is what I want to do—I decide to let it slide. Then out of like nowhere I ask him if he's ever seen a girl naked before, which I figure he probably hasn't because of his age and the fact that he's so much of a pussy in general. "Sure," he tells me. "Of course I've seen a naked girl before."

"Who?" I'm laughing when I say it. On purpose. "Who was it, you pussy?"

"Lots of girls you wouldn't even know. I saw a girl from my old neighborhood naked. I used to have a girlfriend."

"Of course you did," I tell him. "All the squirrels in DC let you see them naked, I bet. And they're all hot too, right? And they let you fuck them. And you're good at it. Tell me, Donny . . ." I call him Donny because I know he hates being called that. "Did this girlfriend of yours have a nice fuzzy BEAVER to look at? Did she let you get up close to it? Did it bite?"

His face goes all red when I say "BEAVER." It's awesome. Except I actually feel a little bad for embarrassing him. But, fuck it. He sucks, right?

Donald doesn't know how to respond. He decides to whine at me. "Shut uuuuuup," he goes in this goofy drawn-out squeal. "I have *too* seen one." He starts nodding. Rapidly. I thought his head would fall off. "It was a nice one," he says. "*Really* nice."

"Well what did it look like then?"

"Just, you know . . . a . . . *hole*," he says.

I want to smack him. "An a-hole?" I ask. "Psych. Just a hole, huh?"

"Yup. A hole." He's trying to sound more confident now.

"Did it look like a hole for mice?" I ask him. "Or a hole for rabbits?"

"Neither . . ." He seems confused. "Um, mice, I guess."

"That's not what the vaginas I've seen look like," I tell him. "They don't look like holes that mice would live in to me."

"Well what do they look like then? If you know so much about them . . ."

"They look like roast beef," I tell him. "The rare stuff. And they smell like tuna."

"No they don't," he goes. "Prove it."

"Go ask your mother," I tell him.

~

It's not like I even know anything about vaginas from personal experience. I'm not some kind of PUSSY EXPERT or anything. I've never even fingered anybody yet, even though I have gotten a hand job on the bus ride to a ski trip in Vermont with this youth group my mother sometimes sends me to now because she feels bad that us kids never went to church, mostly on account of being lazy but also because of my dad's atheism.

I've seen plenty of porno movies though and it's not like I don't have the Internet. So I pretty much know all the ins and outs of that area of the female anatomy, if you know what I'm saying. I've seen pretty far up in there and besides the smell which I've heard rumors about but cannot exactly confirm, I think I know about what to expect . . . But sometimes I wonder if the girls my age will be shaved or not when I get to them. Not that I would put up a fuss either way. I just wonder is all.

~

By the way, have I mentioned that I'm absolutely addicted to animation? I love it. I wish I could draw. Right now there are about a million cartoons on television but most of them are just a lot of that nonsense Japanese shit with the huge eyes and blinking lights and freak out animals and all that other stuff that supposedly causes seizures. It's true there are still a few good cartoons out there like *The Simpsons* and stuff, don't get me wrong, but I like the old shows better. *Tom and Jerry* and Magilla Gorilla and Droopy and Road Runner and shit. Bugs Bunny was my earliest role model. I used to fake his accent.

Come to think of it, I always wanted to live in Cartoonworld. Where the colors are bright and constant and there aren't any little details to get in your way. You can do pretty much whatever you want and nothing can ever really hurt you, not permanently, and your whole life is this sweet-ass cartoon chase game.

Personally, I LOVED being chased as a kid. But I knew that if I was a cartoon, running away would be that much sweeter. I'd never look down when I walked off cliffs, for instance. And it wouldn't even matter if I did. I'd just let the wind whistle past my ears until I turned into a puff of smoke at the bottom of some ghastly ravine. Then I'd get up and start all over again when the stars and little birdies were done orbiting my head. Besides, cartoon girls are way sexy. Being a cartoon would rule. The whole thing would be completely and utterly sweet.

I definitely want to start taking LSD soon or whenever I can find some because I heard that it might make me see cartoons or something like them. Which would be pretty fucking cool even though I doubt if they're going to look exactly the way they do on TV. But anything even remotely close would be cool enough for me. I'd just like the world to get all changed around on me for a while. Into something a bit more interesting. Anything besides plain old real life with its complicated boring everything. I realize that cartoon physics wouldn't actually apply if I took acid, like I wouldn't be able to draw a tunnel on a wall and then run through it and if I stepped off a cliff gravity would pull me down like a stone and maybe even push my bones through my skin on impact. I mean, duh. But I wouldn't mind if things got a little animated around here for a while. Even if it was just on the surface.

~

I'm upstairs right now listening to a punk rock song about panty raids on my boom box because my mother is downstairs running the vacuum. I have the volume up really loud. All my mother ever does is clean. And smoke her cigarettes and sip her light beers and go to work every day, especially now. She bought my sisters a cat this spring to keep at her house, even though she is allergic. So now she cleans even more with the cat around, but also I think she does it because she's nervous. My mom's a very nervous person. And she likes things to be clean.

Cleaning up after the cat makes her even more allergic because she scrubs things on her hands and knees. That means she has to get down all close to the dander. I tell her this sometimes. But she doesn't listen. I don't like watching her on her hands and knees. I didn't used to mind, but now it bugs me for some reason. I feel bad for her. I wish I was older and rich and could pay for someone to take care of her. Besides, I think all the cleaning noises—the faucet, the vacuum, the scrubbing, the dishes—are extremely fucking annoying, especially if I'm trying to watch TV. So I just lock myself in the bedroom when she starts cleaning. And turn on really loud music.

The cat himself doesn't bother me. I'd kind of like having him around if it wasn't for my mother's sneezing and coughing and the way her face sometimes gets all puffy and swollen. Seeing her like that makes me feel bad. I wish she could be more comfortable. But I don't blame the cat for it. He never asked to live here.

~

My little sisters are twins, but they dye their hair and dress differently so they can tell themselves apart. Both of them love to gossip and spy. They're actually not that much younger than me, only one and a half years, but at that age you're still sort of a kid anyway. I mean, they haven't stopped writing in cursive for chrissakes.

Well, last night I barged into the room they share at my mother's house. Mainly because I was stuck in a video game and bored to death, but also because there were these wild giggling sounds coming from behind their door and I wanted to see what was so funny. I popped the lock on their door with a paper clip, which is a cinch on the cheap locks inside both my folks' houses. I threw open the door and stood there with my arms folded across my chest like Mister Clean.

They didn't notice me at first. They had all the lights turned off and were rolling around on the floor by the window. So I flicked on the lights. They looked up at me, frozen like a pair of startled rodents.

Their faces were bright red. They were sweating. Panting. Littering the carpet around them was all sorts of equipment: flashlights, hand mirrors, a pair of binoculars, a magnifying glass. I just waited in the doorway, looking down on them.

"We're spying," Katie went as soon as she caught her breath. "We think there's a killer living across from us. Over there. At the end of that row. Where the show house used to be."

I took up the binoculars and sat on the edge of my sister's bed. I looked out the window through a crack in the blinds. All of the houses are designed to look exactly alike. It was dark out. There was nothing to see but moths banging themselves against the streetlight.

"I don't see anything," I mumbled, holding the binoculars to my face.

"Well, there's a killer. And Katie has the hots for him. She's into bad boys . . ."

They started cackling and rolling around the floor again. Laughing until there wasn't even any sound coming from their lips. They were shaking.

After they got a hold of themselves, Katie wiped the corner of her eye with a sigh. "Ewww. Stop it, Kelly. That's gross. He's like ninety."

I called them both ridiculous.

"Fine," Kelly *umphed*. "Ignore the fact that we're living across the street from a psychopath. Me and Mom and Katie can handle the murderer ourselves. It's not like we expect *you* to protect us."

"Yeah. It's not like you're the man of the house or anything . . ."

I cut them off. "What makes you think this geezer is anything but a boring old turd? Why were you even spying on him?"

"Well, we were originally watching this really hot guy from across the street and he's like in his thirties but Katie wants to marry him anyway and . . ."

"I do *not*," whined Katie.

"Do too. Anyway, this guy lives two doors down from the old dude—the Killer—and he drives the coolest BMW SUV . . ."

"The old man?" I found myself asking, actually curious.

"No! The hottie. But anyway Katie was practically drooling on the window . . ."

"You were, too!"

"Fine. We were both totally drooling. But then we saw this gross old guy that lives at the end of the row. He pulled up in that disgusting Honda . . ." Kelly pointed out the window at a Civic hatchback squatted up against the curb like a tired old bulldog. She scoffed. "It looks like a cockroach," she said.

"And when he got out he looked around all sketchy like someone was watching him . . ."

"And then we saw him take out this huge, like, duffel bag . . ."

"It was a body bag!"

"Yeah. A *body bag*. And he carried it over his shoulder, looking all squirrelly and nervous . . . And the bag was moving." Kelly paused. She was thinking about something. "Freaky," she said, biting her lip.

"It was sketchy," Katie agreed, slowly nodding her head. They both looked deadly serious.

I peered through the binoculars again, this time looking directly at the old man's house but the drapes were pinched shut. There was a sort of reddish light coming from inside the curtains. That's weird, I thought, everyone else in this community has Venetian blinds.

~

"*Stop staring at me, Mom,*" I whine over the sound of the television. "I can feel it." My sisters are outside running around with a bunch of the brats that live around Roland Park Northway. My mother has been in the kitchen since we got home, smoking cigarettes in front of the evening news and talking on the phone about a problem with the computers down at her work. After she gets off she comes halfway into the so-called family room and just stands there watching me with this loony smile eased across her face. I glance up at her out the corner of my eye and then look back at the television. I try to focus. I can't. Even though I probably shouldn't care whether she watches me or not if it makes her happy. Especially since I'm not even *do*ing anything, just lying on the couch in a practice jersey. But I really can feel her eyes on me. It makes it hard to concentrate on the television, although I'm not actually watching anything in particular. "Seriously," I go. "I can feel it."

"Oh my, I'm sorry," she laughs at herself with this cute little shrug, like her right hand just caught her left hand stealing. Then she goes back into the kitchen and I hear her turn on the stove to light a cigarette.

But a few minutes later I can feel her watching me again. I don't even have to look to know she is there. I can just tell. I change the channel a few times. I pretend not to notice. It takes less than a minute before I can't handle it anymore. I fake sleep. I slip my head behind one of the couch cushions, which my mom knows I do for real sometimes when I want to sleep. I lie perfectly still like that. Pretend she's not there. After a few minutes I hear her cough and she asks me if I'd maybe like to visit the zoo with her sometime soon. I keep quiet and pretend I'm asleep. I can tell she is still there. Watching me. Eventually I start to make snoring noises.

~

I have this booklist I'm supposed to read by the end of the summer to get ready for my freshman year in high school. They sent out this letter that says I'm supposed to be tested or something. And I have to write a personal essay about myself. My past and future, hopes and regrets, all that kind of bullshit. See, I'm signed up to start at this lousy Catholic high school in Towson where I won't know anybody in my class except for this one greaseball from the school I went to last year and, whatever, I try not to think about it. I've changed schools like three times in three and a half years so it's not that big of a deal or anything to be going someplace new. Besides, this school I'm going to next year starts in the ninth grade so everybody in the whole freshman class is kind of the new kid. But seriously, fuck this reading list I have to go through. *Lord of the Flies* for one thing sounds like a book on mosquito abatement. Which might be kind of cool actually, now that I think about it . . .

~

Since I've switched schools so often in the last few years I've had to make friends at each one and now it's like I have multiple sets of friends or acquaintances or whatever you want to call them, all from different neighborhoods and like social classes. For example, the city school I went to in seventh grade was what's called a "magnet school." The kids came from all over the city, so there was a metal detector at the door and we were required to wear clear plastic book bags. Everybody was black for the most part except me. And this kid in the grade above me that became my friend. His name is Robby, but he calls himself the Beaster Bunny. We still hang out sometimes. He sells me weed. The Beaster Bunny lives near my dad's place on the edge of Homeland and the black neighborhood next door called Govans, which is where my mother grew up before what I've heard my dad refer to as "white flight" started happening.

Before I went to city school, I did elementary at this ultra-wealthy private school in Guilford that's been around for like more than two hundred years or something. The teachers hated me there. Really. *Hated* me. Even though I was just a little kid. They thought I was out of control or something. The kids liked me all right though. That's where people started calling me Retard. Most of them were jerks from either Roland Park or Homeland or Ruxton or Guilford, which are all very nice neighborhoods with mansions full of monogrammed silver and whale print ottomans and Labrador retrievers. Everyone was blond or had freckles. There was also a contingent of rich kids that rode in every day in this cheesebox school bus from out in the valley. That school was pretty far from what you might call diverse. Everybody was practically related. That's how it is in Baltimore.

And most recently, like just this spring even, I was going to a small Catholic middle school on Harford Road. That's in east Baltimore. Some of my cousins who are older went there before me and that was how come I knew about the place. It was probably why they accepted me too, especially considering that it was past the registration date when I started there last fall.

The school was attached to this little church in Hamilton where my grandparents used to go, back when they were still alive. Hamilton is a lot different than where I live, but it's kind of cool too, with gritty sidewalks and vinyl-sided front porches and nearby is this nursing home full of loonies who hang out at the bus stop outside Dunkin' Donuts with chocolate all over their faces. All the other kids in my class were parishioners and I'd never really been to much church until I went there, which felt kind of weird in a way. I was like the only kid who wasn't going to confirmation classes, which is apparently where a lot of the action was happening. Whatever. I just graduated last week. I wonder if I'll ever see the kids in my class again, since it was kind of far away. See, I had to take a long ride on the MTA bus to get home every day. But that turned out all right because the bus trip usually gave me a lot of time to think about stuff. Or zone out at least.

I have to zone out after school. Or take a nap. Going to school makes my eyeballs hurt. Not the lights or anything. Just school in general. And it ends up sucking wherever you go I figure . . . except maybe college, which probably sucks just as bad but in a different way. And I'm not sure I want to go that route anyhow so I doubt I'll ever find out. It's not just the waking up early or the homework or teachers or bullies or geeks that make school suck in my opinion. Not that my opinion matters or anything since you have to go to school no matter what, but *still* . . . The way I see it, all that stuff is just DETAILS. What's really important, what I think sucks the most about school, is what it does to your time. It KILLS it. Just the fact that you have to be there fucking blows. Being a REQUIREMENT makes the whole thing feel like a giant weight on a kid's back. I hook school a lot. These are supposed to be the best years of my life, aren't they? Why shouldn't I be absolutely free to enjoy every second of it the way I want? Isn't time the most valuable thing a person can own? Isn't it the only thing? That's why I say, fuck school. Because life is too precious. What if I were to die tomorrow? All I'd know is long division and maybe a couple prayers in Latin. And how to read. Fuck all that, you know what I mean? I think it's a shame that time is so costly, but what are you gonna do? And now my mom keeps reminding me of this booklist I've got to worry about . . . And that essay. About me, Retard, of all things . . .

~

This morning I woke up feeling all sticky and faded from this doozy of a fucked up dream that was banging all around my head last night. The dream was a fleeting one, running away all fast like WOOSH! as I sat up in bed. But I still remember part of it. About an infestation of bunny rabbits. The rabbits only came out at night. I was at this impossibly enormous resort with my family but it was also a school maybe and a summer camp and a city all in one. There were a ton of people I knew there, but also a lot of strangers. The locals were scared of these rabbits I think.

Anyway I was sticky and faded when I woke up, but I didn't feel like taking a shower yet. I was at my dad's house, so I picked up a towel and wandered up to the community pool. The sun was high already and the glare dodged in and out between the rows of houses, blocking off spots of my vision. I kept thinking about my dream. It began to fall apart even more as I thought about it. I walked up the middle of the road and the pavement was hot on my feet.

When I got to the pool I walked right past the sign-in sheet on the faux-wood table by the gate and dropped my towel on the nearest chair without looking at anybody. Then I went over to the deep end, still not looking left or right, and dove in. I nearly lost my shorts in the water but managed to catch them from behind by the waistband, thank god. I came up blinking and went back under. I swam froggy-style to the steps in the shallow end. I sat down and leaned back against the metal handrail. It was hot on my shoulder and felt good. I ran my fingers through my hair. I thought about shaving it off.

See, I usually try not to make eye contact with anybody at first when I get to the pool, especially if I'm all by myself, because I never know who will be there or whatever and I guess I'm secretly shy underneath or something. I mean mostly it's just old people and some gay dudes lounging around and a few little kids maybe or divorcees, but there are also sometimes one or two pretty good-looking females there on occasion. And the community is only halfway built right now anyway, so there are new people moving in all the time. I always bring a towel or at least a T-shirt to the pool so I can cover up in case I get a boner, which is something that could basically happen at the drop of a hat. Anyway, because of all this, I never know who to make eye contact with and shit like that. So I usually try to avoid the situation completely and just head straight for the deep end.

Well, today that meant I didn't notice where my sisters had stationed themselves: right behind the steps I was sitting on in the shallow end, where the sun's rays were hitting the hardest. I heard them giggling behind me and in that same second I felt something cold and greasy hit the back of my neck with a fart. Suntan lotion. Without looking behind me or saying anything at all, I waded forward into the pool until the water was up to my chin and the gob of lotion started to peel off and break up in the water. I dunked my head underneath, planning to create a tremendous splash in the direction of the steps when I resurfaced, looking for a revenge by dowsing. I hooked my fingers together like a basket and pushed off the cement bottom. A monster clear-blue fan of chlorine rose up from the pool. I watched the wave, laughter already dripping off my lips as it broke up in the air.

That's when I noticed my sisters were now standing a good ways off, watching me from a few rows back. They had their towels, bags, cell phones, and lotion gripped to their chests and these toothy fucking grins on their faces. My heart dropped into my stomach. See, right in front of where my sisters were standing, between two empty chairs, was the dirty blonde hair, smoothly arched spine, and tiny round buttocks of Ashley Vidal. She had her headphones on. She must've been lying between those two sneaky bitches, sleeping, when they pulled their prank. I flung my arms to catch the droplets as they fell. Kelly and Katie laughed even harder.

Ashley Vidal is this girl who lives in my father's neighborhood with her mother and her little brother Kevin. Kevin is nine years old and likes to station himself by the entrance to the pool sometimes and put on puppet shows dramatizing hip-hop's most infamous beefs. It's kind of funny. Anyway, since Ashley's only twelve years old and closer to my sisters' age and a girl, she became one of *their* new best friends this spring after she moved into a house near the front gate. Because of this, she did *not* become one of MY new best friends. Which is too fucking bad because, no lie, she is like the hottest thing in the entire fucking galaxy. ALREADY. And she's only TWELVE YEARS OLD!!!

Now, I know, I'm only fourteen myself, right? But I'll be fifteen this fall (Halloween, bitch! BOO!) and in high school and even though I'm not that much older than Ashley Vidal, she still seems kind of young. Like a kid. Except for the fact that she already has these perfect little titties growing out of her chest. And her nipples are almost always rock hard. She never even lets on. She's oblivious. Which might have something to do with the spaced-out look that's perpetually on her face. Like her head is full of helium and could float away at any moment. Plus, she has this flawless jawline and puffy lips and the cutest little scar under her left eye, which I would totally pretend I'd never, ever, ever noticed before if anyone found a reason to ask me about it. Anyway, moral of the story is basically that a blind man could see that not only is this girl super fucking hot but she is about to get super, incredibly fucking hot over the next few years. Like she's growing into her body or something. So my goal in life right now is to get in on the ground floor with her. Except I'm too lazy and way too much of a pussy to do anything about it . . .

Well, Ashley woke up when I splashed her. Her perfect mouth was shocked wide open and her sunglasses had fallen off. I remember a kind of like mist over her eyes from sleeping. It went away in a flash. Like I'd pulled her through a crack in the side of a giant egg. I felt pretty bad about splashing her. My sisters were giggling in the background like tiny dogs and that seemed to heighten the effect. I got angry. Instead of apologizing like I should have, I pointed over Ashley's shoulder at my sisters, yelling, "THEIR FAULT! THEIR FAULT! FUCK YOU GUYS! I HATE YOU!" But Ashley was still wearing headphones, so I doubt if she heard me.

Secretly humiliated, I cussed my sisters. I shook my fist at them, kicking backwards toward the deep end with this hollow feeling in my chest. I climbed out of the pool and marched over to my chair and sat down to dry myself off. I desperately wondered if anyone was staring at me. But I was too terrified to even look up and see. And I was too proud to storm off. So I ended up lying in the sun with a towel over my face until it seemed appropriate—four and a half minutes exactly, I counted the seconds—before getting up. I headed back to my dad's. I made a bong from an empty milk carton and smoked it by the window with my Froot Loops. But the first thing I did when I got inside was make sure to lock all the doors, knowing my sisters probably hadn't taken a key.

~

The difference between my two sisters is hard to define exactly, but I'll try as best I can. Here goes: Katie is a Bryn Mawr girl. Kelly goes to Roland Park Country. They mostly have the same friends, a lot of whom go to Maryvale or Cathedral or Garrison Forest or St. Paul's. Kelly's hair is dyed about the color of a wet dog, while Katie's hair is shiny platinum blonde at the moment. Katie's initials are KAL, while Kelly's initials happen to spell out her nickname, KEL, a coincidence I'm not sure she's moved past bragging about yet. While both girls share musical tastes (whatever's on MTV) they usually end up leaning slightly toward opposing sides of the dial in terms of style and whatnot—like, if it's hip-hop and wuss rock on the pop charts this week, Kelly will be slightly more of a rocker chick and Katie will try to play up the urban look or vice versa, in order to avoid confusing people. Kelly still has a thumb-sucking problem that's resulted in a slight overbite for which she uses a retainer and Katie has just undergone hypnosis for her nail-biting habit. (I have the same oral fixation and scabs on my cuticles, but you don't see me complaining.) When we're driving with my father, Kelly always calls shotgun and usually gets it based on a phony complaint about the back seat giving her motion sickness. Katie, on the other hand, is constantly whining for foot rubs. Neither girl is a genius but they both get pretty good grades. A lot better than me at least.

If they ever had one of those secret twin languages, I never picked up on it. But they do spend enough time together that everyone in north Baltimore says their names in one breath, like they're a brokerage firm or something. Kelly & Katie, Inc. or whatever. I guess that's sort of inevitable when you're somebody's twin.

When I was a kid I used to wonder if maybe I had a twin brother somewhere, especially after I learned that twinnage is something you get from genetics and family history. I figured I might have one too. Why not, right? It was stupid, I know, but I used to pretend that he might be out there, with some crazy life maybe. Like sold into slavery on a pirate ship in the Indian Ocean. Or just super mega-rich somewhere, like the adopted son of a sterile but very cool Powerball winner in search of an heir or something. It seemed like a pretty sweet idea at the time, something to hope for. Maybe we could find each other someday and discover we had something MAGIC in common, like a sixth sense or a recurring dream that would connect us immediately even though we had been strangers all our lives. We'd even have the same birthmark! It'd be like a fucking movie! But then I thought, what if we had nothing in common but our winespot? What if he was good at things? What if we HATED each other?

Around that same time—I was just a little guy when all this was going down in my noggin—I learned about cloning and thought that might be a better alternative to having a twin. A clone, or a bunch of them, exactly like you in every way at birth, I thought, HOW WONDERFUL! You could be best friends with them or not, depending on how you felt. Like you could write your clone occasionally to exchange insights on your personal life, insights that only a clone would have. Or you could just be total homeboys with him and hang out all the time. And you could even join up with your clones and live together in groups to form a super-efficient TEAM CLONE, like if you were a brilliant scientist or Michael Jordan or something. Just think of the possibilities . . .

But then I realized that even if I were cloned this very second I'd still be a bunch of years older than my clone, so we'd never really look exactly alike at the same time. I'd always look older and closer to death. It might even be creepy to have one of them hanging around, like looking into a living photograph or a memory of yourself or whatever. And some clones are bound to be more popular than others and shit. That would make me feel pretty bad, I think. If my clone was cooler than me. Really, the more I let myself think about it, the whole idea of duplicates started to depress me.

~

Now, I don't usually believe in god or alien abductions or any of that kind of shit, but a couple of minutes ago I saw some stuff on the television that made me feel pretty confused about history and the meaning of life and everything. It was this show on Discovery or the Learning Channel or National Geographic or some shit (those are like my favorite channels). The show was about these crystal skulls that were discovered in Mexico or someplace. The skulls are see-through and they're supposed to be really, really old. Older than the pyramids or whatever.

Legend has it there are thirteen of them, which is supposed to be this really unlucky number. Only five of the skulls have ever been found though and they're all owned by museums or rich people or whatever, but the legend says that there are eight more out there somewhere. When all the skulls have been uncovered they're supposed to reveal some kind of secret about the universe or something. That's bonkers, I know, and I thought it sounded like bullshit when I first heard it, too.

But what's most crazy about the whole thing is that they had all these scientists on the program talking about how there are no tool markings on the skulls anywhere. They look like they're made out of liquid. Like ice. It's completely unreal. The scientists say the skulls are made out of this very hard kind of silicon that would need to be cut by a diamond or a laser, which would have been impossible for the ancient Mexicans to do, especially without leaving any marks.

What's more, the legend says the skulls are supposed to contain all this important information inside, and the scientists say the silicon they're made out of is basically the same shit they make computer chips from. CRAZY, right? And so all these people are out there looking all over the damn continent for the other eight skulls. The five that have been discovered were each found in different parts of

Latin America, not even all that close to one another. But the legend says that the skulls cannot be found until the human race is completely ready and only then will we be able to learn the secrets inside. But all these people are out there looking for them anyway, searching and searching. Figuring I guess that we're ready enough as it is.

~

The truth is, I've never really been all that sexy of a dude. Not sexy like handsome (although probably not that either, on account of my blotchy right eye), but sexy like horny or whatever, I mean. I'm not even all that into porno for instance, even though I've seen plenty of it. Mostly I just watch it with my friends out of curiosity and stuff, sort of the same way I used to look up dirty words in the dictionary during study hall. Just for fun, you know. Just to *see*. Truthfully, I kind of think people fucking look silly, the things they say and the faces they make and noises and all that. It's weird. I don't even use porno when I jerk myself off. More often than not I just use my imagination and stuff. Think about people I know. Like certain teachers or my friends' older sisters and shit. And really the only reason I *do* beat it so much is because I keep getting these random goddamn hard-ons all the time. At the weirdest times. In the car with my mother or during a lacrosse game or something. It's terrible. And then after I blow my load it feels like I HATE sex or something. I can't bring myself to even THINK about whoever I was just beating it to, even if it is someone like Ashley Vidal . . . or Venus . . .

Seriously, no matter what, my crushes just dissolve after masturbating. As soon as that little white gob jumps from the end of my wiener, all I can think of is skateboarding or cartoons or video games or sleep. It's weird. I just feel like the whole thing about sexiness is so overrated. Which is a dumb thing for me to think, I know, especially because I'm a virgin and all. Plus I know in my head that fucking is a natural thing and all animals have to do it to propagate their species, so whatever. But somehow I just can't help thinking it's a pretty stupid activity, which makes me feel a little bit like a freak. Especially since I'm walking around with a big old hard-on tucked up against my belly most of the time.

I just can't help being fascinated by fucking. Even if it does seem kind of stupid or VAPID, which is a sweet new word I just learned. I read it off the liner notes in this punk rock CD I bought and decided to look it up. It was being used as this guy's last name, the guitarist or whatever, and even though he was using it as a name, I could tell it was a real word. A lot of punk rock guys adopt real words as last names, just because they sound cool and make good aliases or whatever. My real last name is a word already, LOVER, you know, but I never thought it sounded that cool. Anyhow, I looked up the word "vapid" in the dictionary and it sort of means dumb and boring and like, *dead*, you know. And sometimes I think all that sexy stuff seems kind of like that. Vapid or whatever. But on the other hand I want to get laid as soon as possible if I can. I'd probably do just about anything to make it happen. Really, I mean it, probably anything in the world . . .

~

I was all vegged out in front of the TV in my mother's basement next to Thomas Angel the cat, who has two names on account of my mother allowing my sisters to name him and them not being able to decide on just one. I was surfing past one of those health channels that usually showcase all these nasty close-ups of surgical operations and shit, when I saw a program coming up next that grabbed my attention. The program was called *Boy Expires.* It was about this thirteen-year-old boy who just like DIED for no reason the doctors could figure out except apparently his time was up. Well that threw me for a goddamn loop all right! What do they mean, *expires*? Like milk? I didn't understand. Well just as I was getting ready to find out, my mother's doorbell rang and I went to open it and Gary and John were standing there with their mountain bikes resting against their hips, waiting. I guess they had been at Gary's house because he lives not too far away on Club Road in Roland Park. John lives all the way out off of Falls Road past St. Paul's in a subdivision called Pine Ridge Terrace or Pine Terrace Green or something. All the houses are these mammoth cube-shaped things made out of beige-colored bricks with huge perfectly distributed backyards. Everything in the neighborhood looks pretty much the same because it was all built at the same time by the same company. On top of somebody's farm or something. I hate that shit. All those cheesy new houses out there, they make me sick. They're so unoriginal. They bore me. Which is a kind of weird thing for me to say because both of my parents' subdivisions are sort of like that too, except they're townhomes instead of mansions and they're still technically in the city and all.

Anyway, they wanted me to go out and ride bikes around Homeland. Truthfully, what I really wanted to do was figure out what caused the boy on TV to expire, it seemed important somehow to find out. But instead, I pussied out and went with them anyway. I've never been able to say no to anybody.

It's not that I don't like hanging out with John or Gary. I do. I've known them both forever. Ever since we used to go to the same preppy-ass fucking grade school and play rec league lax and shit. It's just that I don't really enjoy hanging out with them *together* anymore, you know what I mean? Just one or the other is fine. But when they're both together I usually feel like they're making fun of me. Like I'll innocently say something, anything, something that would probably go over pretty well if it was just one of them with me. But if it's both of them they'll look at each other and smirk like I'm a dork or an idiot or something, cut me down like some oddball annoyance. Things get all antagonistic with them. It makes me feel bad about myself. Like I ought to reach out and break their teeth or whatever. Which I never do because I'm a total wuss.

For instance, today when we were riding out of my mother's community, I noticed this old Honda hatchback pull up. Out climbs the old man my sisters have been spying on, the Killer and all. Only this time he wasn't alone. He was with this young black chick. She had a cool little moustache and acid-washed jeans decorated with stars and hearts and shit going all up and down her thighs in glitter that sparkled when the sun hit it just right. They were unloading two-by-fours and a big bag of wood chips from his car. Well, I thought that was pretty weird. That these two very different people were hanging out and working on a project together I mean. Not her jeans or the woodchips especially. Just the whole situation in general. I thought it was interesting.

The Spring Lakes are these six artificial ponds on Springlake Way in Homeland, which are full of carp and crayfish and kind of pretty too even though they're fake. When we got there, I told Gary and John the story about how my sisters had been spying on the old man and how they thought he was a killer and how I had just seen him kicking it with a young-looking black chick in glittery jeans and all. I guess I took a while telling the story—I always take a long time telling people stories because I never know what details they are going to think are the important ones and sometimes they all seem pretty important to me. But I didn't take *that* long and all we were doing was crayfishing with a stupid tree branch anyway, so I thought they'd be pretty interested. It's not like either of them were saying anything too remarkable. And I think they *would* have been pretty interested if they hadn't been together. Or maybe they wouldn't have been interested, but they would've at least *pretended* to be interested. Instead they were all, "Hey, Retard, so-fucking-what?" and "Who cares about some old douchebag anyway?" Which nearly broke my heart, even though I don't even *know* the old guy. It just seemed like he deserved some respect, even if he *was* a killer. Anyway why the fuck did they ride by my house and pick me up if they weren't interested in hearing the kind of things I had to say? To make me feel bad? Fuck all that. Seriously. Fuck those guys.

So we went on scooping up these crunchy green crayfish with a stick. A crayfish is just about the dumbest animal on earth. They're simple to catch. They will just climb up a stick and cling to it if you dip it far enough in the water, you don't even need to bait them or anything. Anyway, that's what we were doing when Gary asked me if I had any pot. I lied and said I was completely dry because well, fuck those guys. I didn't feel like sharing.

We kept on horsing around with the crayfish, like heating them up with a lighter at the foot of this little bronze statue of a nymph standing by the lake. She's wearing an overturned lily as a cap. It looks like she's peeing down her leg . . . Point is, the three of us were just fucking around in general. Daring each other to jump in the water, which wouldn't actually be that bad probably except the Spring Lakes are kind of murky and gross-looking and it's probably illegal to swim in them even though there isn't a sign. Well, while we were fucking around we noticed this crew of black boys in the semi-distance. They were definitely headed up to the lakes, a couple of them on bikes that looked stolen because they were way too small. The rest of them were on foot, moving down the center of the road.

"Holy shit," John squeaked, like he'd seen a shark or something. "Let's get out of here . . ."

Gary agreed with him, looking all serious. "Dude. Nigs. Let's split."

Now, that sort of pissed me off to hear them talk like that. Not the word "nig," that didn't bother me so much, but the two of them being so automatically frightened pissed me off. I mean, they were probably right, these kids weren't going to come up and ask to be our best friends or whatever, but still . . . I know Gary and John well enough to know that they're probably terrified of every black person they meet. After all, there's only a couple of them at their school and there damn sure aren't any of them lying around either of the country clubs those two practically live at come summertime. People that are afraid of everything, especially other people, really piss me off.

Me, I figured I might even *know* one or two of the black kids from going to city school in seventh grade. Which might not be that great of a thing considering one of the major reasons I left before the end of the year was because of all the fistfights I was getting in. But still, I hate it when all the rich kids I grew up with act all ignorant and scared of black people and poor people and the city or whatever. It's like they're brainwashed or something. They're such pussies. Fifty bucks says their kids and their kids' kids will be the same way too. Just because they've never had the balls to sit down and talk to an actual honest-to-god BLACK PERSON. I mean, it's totally fucked up.

I wanted to stay and see what the kids wanted at least, but Gary and John had already started riding off, leaving all these half-dead crayfish squirming and snapping at each other on the little nymph's feet. So I just hopped on my bike and followed them. But I felt like a dipshit for doing it. We spent the next half-hour playing Ding Dong Ditch, which was fun in third grade maybe. It's just lame now. And when we were riding back in the direction of my mom's place Gary asked me if I had any pot—as if he hadn't *just* asked me earlier. So I lied again and said no. They went home after that.

~

When I was just a little guy, I liked myself pretty good until I realized that nobody else particularly liked me. Then I tried to change so people would like me better. Once that happened, I could like myself again. I thought it worked for a while. People started to like me all right and I thought I could enjoy my own company again. But sometimes I'm not so sure.

~

Thomas Angel brought home a mouse today. He left it on the doorstep at my mother's. It was my job to get rid of it. I didn't complain.

~

One of my father's biggest beefs when we were all living at my old house, bigger than my report card or getting brought home by the fuzz (I'll tell you some more stories later . . . I was on probation all last year . . . I do everything wrong . . .), bigger than anything really, was when skateboards got ridden in the house. Which happened a lot. This was the all-time worst sin I guess and when he heard me even just flipping my board in place on the carpet downstairs, which was supposed to be our "game room" with a pool table and stuff, my dad would just absolutely FREAK. His screams would echo through the walls all around me and I would wince and look over at my buddy like it was the voice of god yelling for us to be quiet. I'd give my dad the finger through the ceiling as I swore not to do it again. But I've never been able to keep a promise.

Anyway, the hardwood and the moldings and even the roof (which was actually highly skateable in the one or two little areas that weren't made out of slate), they were absolutely sacred to that guy. He was constantly fretting over the condition of the house, the amount of clutter, the lawn. I don't think anything ever got *too* fucked up anyway. I mean who cares if it looks like somebody lives there, a family for chrissakes. He was always just bugging out in general over all the most unimportant shit. He refused to build me a treehouse because of the way it would look in the neighborhood, even though there was a nice-sized possum nest made out of brambles and garbage in one of our trees by the road.

He never let me build skate ramps for the same reason. They were ugly. In his opinion, they had to be ugly, despite the fact that my father was an excellent carpenter who made his own bookshelves and a bench for the breakfast nook. Ironically, a backyard mini is probably about the only thing that would've kept me from skating in the house! My dad let us have a backyard lacrosse goal because, well, everyone in this part of town has one, but he hated the idea of a trampoline. Even though my sisters wanted one too. He was worried it would kill a patch in the lawn. It's not like he was scared for our safety on any of these things. I had BB guns and a Buck knife and shit. He used to take me rock climbing and skiing. He dropped me off at the skate park all the time without a helmet. I was ALLOWED to build a rope swing.

But now I realize the reason he was so anal about the house was because he knew all along that we weren't going to be there forever. He's in real estate for chrissakes. It's easy to take down a fucking rope swing. You just cut it off.

So what I knew as an ivy-covered paradise full of potential—this place that could be added to and customized on and on forever—my father saw as an investment. Insurance against bad times to come. Now I realize that's why we had that useless fucking exercise room off of the basement—a room that could have housed a ramp or was maybe even going to be my bedroom at one point. It's because potential buyers like to see what that part of the house would look like as a stupid exercise room, because that's what kind of room they would probably have if they lived there. It was a display. A prop. As if there aren't enough unused workout rooms out there, full of gadgets for people who can't figure out how to use their muscles. Like these people can't come up with a physical activity more stimulating than walking up and down on a machine that simulates a fucking staircase . . .

Workout rooms really make me sick, by the way. I can't think of anything more boring than a room you exercise in. Why don't people just go and DO something once in a while if they want to shed pounds? Explore. Climb a tree. Get in a fistfight. Whatever. What do they need a conveyer belt and a room full of mirrors for? It's so ignorant. Anyway, we used to have a workout room in the basement. Strictly for fucking show.

It pisses me off that my dad was planning on leaving that house all along, ever since he bought it. Not that I blame him. I mean he did pay for it and all that. But it pisses me off that I could go for so long, thinking all the time—even when they'd get separated and stuff because my mother would always stay at home and my room would never change or anything—that we would live in our house forever, that maybe I would even own the old homestead one day. And then my son after me. How retarded is that? I'm so stupid . . .

The house really is in a swell location by the way, at the very top of the city on Charles Street, which is like the main vein running through Baltimore. It's the road that separates everything into east and west. I always thought that was cool when I was a kid. East and West.

But seriously, that place would be sweet to live in one day when I'm some old dude, I imagine. It was built by a man and woman who raised six children, four of them hearing-impaired, and then grew old together and died. Although I'm not sure whether they died in the house or not. Or together, at the same time either. That would be weird if they had. My father told me the old man had a big-ass train set in the basement at the open house, but train sets are stupid. I would have a half pipe and a treehouse and a trampoline and a rocking chair and a four-foot hookah pipe. Maybe even a hound dog and a shotgun—even though I probably couldn't shoot it around here without seeing the inside of the clink. It's illegal to discharge firearms within city limits. But maybe I could hang a great big flag, with my face on it, flying over the roof in the wind. It would be perfect. But it'll never happen. Not now. It's like no one respects anything anymore.

~

While Katie and Kelly were at summer league practice this afternoon, I moseyed into their bedroom with an eye out for extra money. I owed the $$$ to Tobin Detzer, who had sold me some of his mother's Xanax. I found three dollars in change lying around Katie's old dollhouse. I went over to their desk drawers to look for some real, paper money. Eventually I found Kelly's wallet. There was fifty bucks inside. I only took five.

As I was turning around to leave I noticed the binoculars lying in a mess of magazines decorated with glitter-paint doodles, signatures and flowers and boy's names and stuff. Technically they're my binoculars, even though I never use them. I picked them up off the ground so they wouldn't get broken. Holding them, I got the urge to look through the lenses. I glanced out the window, but there was nothing to see. I watched a squirrel hop across the rooftops and into the big oak tree. For a second I thought he might slip through the branches, they were bending so much under the weight of his leap. But he made it all right. Squirrels never fall. Or I've never seen one at least. That might be the sort of thing that doesn't happen when there are people around to see it . . .

Near the tree, I noticed the curtains were open on the second floor of the show house where the supposed killer had moved in. I watched a minute until the geezer came into view. He was wearing goggles, an apron, and work gloves. He looked sweaty and frustrated, sinister even. He was holding a hacksaw. I put the binoculars down and stepped away from the window. I didn't want him to see me. Probably nothing, I told myself on the way out. Then I paused by the door and went back in. I went back to Kelly's wallet and took another five.

~

Never in life have I been able to suck a lollipop down into nothingness. I always bite it and break it in pieces in my mouth. I've been trying as long as I can remember. I guess I've never had even a little bit of what you'd call patience or discipline. I flush toilets prematurely, midstream while pissing, out of nervousness. And then I have to wait until the tank refills so I can flush the leftover bubbles. It's embarrassing. And when I was a kid I couldn't stand watching my mother talk on the phone. "Five more minutes," she always said, me tugging on her pant leg and winding myself up in the curlicue phone cord and shit. Then I'd wait a million hours every evening just for my father to get home from his office downtown. And when it rained the streets took forever to dry out so I could skate. Like time was always cheating me somehow.

It cheated in bigger ways too. Holidays never came on time and they rushed past like airplanes out the sunroof when they did. There was always something like five years between Christmas and my birthday. I could never understand why parties and things had to be separated by time to become special. I guess time has that effect on things.

Time moves faster now. Sometimes it moves too fast. I can feel myself getting older. Time has always been a weight on my shoulders in one way or another. I can't get away from it. Nothing I can do. Like I'm stuck in it, chained and smothered by time. It's crazy, right? You can't stop thinking about it. You can't escape. And adults always seem so fucking comfortable with the way time is passing. If anybody should be worried about how time is moving for themselves personally—and I'm pretty sure we should ALL be worried—then it's the adults that should worry. I mean, they are that much closer to death. Think about it.

I think about old Death a lot. Mostly about the death of my parents though. Not my own. I don't spend very much time thinking about my own death, only I always hoped it would happen before my folks had time to kick the bucket—especially my mother. So I don't have to be there or anything. I'd rather die first than watch her go. Most definitely. I know it's selfish, but that's what I hope. I guess I could be a better kid in the meantime. But FUCK TIME, I guess is what I'm saying. I wish I could just forget about it.

So lately I'm terrified of wasting too much time, instead of being bored and wishing the shit would move faster. But that's only because I'm getting older probably. And it doesn't really matter anyway because the effect is still the same either way. Both ways of looking at it make me feel fucking impatient. Both sides of the coin are dirty. I'll probably never finish an entire lollipop without biting it and breaking it in pieces. I envy people that do.

~

My mother tends to cough in her sleep. She isn't that loud, but sometimes I hear her and it wakes me up. Usually I'm already awake watching TV or pulling my dick or whatever . . . I'm a total insomniac . . . And I get scared, listening to her coughs. I wish she wouldn't smoke so much.

But I hate myself for bugging my mom about quitting smoking or about cutting back at least, especially because I smoke cigarettes myself and pot too and sometimes I even smoke my mom's cigarettes when she's not looking and I don't have any of my own. But I figure that Mom's way older and has been smoking forever and smoking like more than a pack of reds a day, which are practically the worst for you except the unfiltered shit. See, I figure I'm better off since I'm young and I smoke light cigarettes and I don't smoke anywhere near as compulsively as she does anyway. I'm probably going to quit sometime in the future, too. I'm only a kid. Smoking could just turn out to be a phase or whatever.

I try not to nag her about her habit. I hate it when she nags me about stuff like wearing shoes outside or waking up for school on time or chewing my food. Nagging is shitty. But I always end up nagging her anyway. I can't help it. I mean, I don't even think nagging works. We should all just leave each other alone and everything would be copacetic, right?

But then again, I hate the sound of her coughing at night. I tear out my skater cut all the time worrying about what it's going to be like to see her rotting away one day with an evil black cancer inside her chest . . . I seriously imagine this stuff. Like holding her hand next to her deathbed as she's on her way out. Me hugging her tiny shoulders till I can feel the bones rub together. Her telling me how wherever I go she'll always be in my heart. Whatever that means. I picture myself smiling into her faded eyes. Trying to act like we've spent enough time together. Quality time. Time in general. I really do imagine this stuff. I miss her like torture already. I can't help it. It's pretty grim. I know I should be enjoying our time together while we have it. Live life. I know that's the most logical thing. Which is why I get so mad at myself for bugging her about smoking and also for being so nasty all the time when she bugs me about my shit. But my mom can get REALLY ANNOYING is all.

Last week I was up the street from my dad's, at the Rite Aid on York Road next to Corky's, when something in the medicine aisle caught my eye. Nico-Water, it was called. Now, my father has gotten my mom both the gum and the patch in the past but I don't think she ever really used them, so I don't know why I thought Nico-Water would work. But whatever, I was interested. Nicotine-infused water. It seemed so cool, you know, futuristic. I had to get it for her.

First I thought about stealing the water. But it came in packages of five that would be kind of hard to stuff down my shorts if you know what I mean. Besides, there was this fake-ass flashlight cop stationed at the entrance of the store. On account of York Road being kind of hood and all. There's always all these wanted posters hanging on a corkboard when you walk into Rite Aid. Which is pretty cool in a way. Like the Wild West.

Anyway, they wouldn't sell me the stuff because it had nicotine in it. Even though it's just water. You can't smoke it or anything. "But I'm trying to quit," I told the bitch at the register, whose Day-Glo press-ons were like three inches long. "Cut a kid a break why don't ya?" I gave her this really sincere kind of look, which *was* real because I meant it. Only I meant it for my mother. Not me. The checkout bitch kind of looked around a second like maybe she was going to sell me the stuff. But then she didn't. Probably because she was scared of being fired and all. I can't blame her for that.

On the way home I decided I'd have to play Hey Mister if I wanted to get that nicotine H_2O. Which was totally gonna suck since it already cost like twenty-eight dollars for five bottles of fucking WATER. Outrageous, right? And it probably wouldn't last my mom more than a day or two anyway. I didn't exactly feel like paying the extra five or ten dollars to have a homeless buy it for me. But if Mom could only try this stuff, I thought. See what it's like not to have the cravings, see how easy it is, then maybe she'd want to quit on her own. I wanted her to quit for herself, you know. Not me. That seemed important at the time.

So today I rode my bike over and parked it at my dad's house. I walked up Homeland Avenue to York Road. My mother had left a pair of crisp twenties on the table this morning for me and my sisters. Pizza, I guess, and maybe a movie rental. I rent a lot of movies. I tore up the note that was sitting alongside the money so my sisters wouldn't find it and know I'd gypped them out of their share. I let the note fall in little pieces along the road on my way. The little pieces looked like flower petals, drifting into the gutter.

It took less than fifteen minutes in broad daylight for a haggard-looking black dude with crusty, wrinkled fingers and bright red eyeballs like Christmas lights to shuffle up and ask if he could help me. I was that obvious. There are like three liquor stores on this one city block and I'm a little white kid. Well, the hobo was pretty fucking confused when I told him what I actually wanted. His eyes kind of rolled around in their sockets. I had to look away.

I was mortified trying to explain myself. I said the water was for me. I said I'd been smoking for years. I'd tried everything. Nothing worked. The only way to quit was the water. "I need it!" I told him. "BAD!" I'm not sure if the dude believed me, but he was all right about it. He thought I was trying to get high with it somehow, I think. This was all just a formality anyway. I ended up paying him the extra ten dollars and he wished me luck. He warned me I was too young to be smoking in the first place. I think it made him feel good to give somebody advice. I didn't want to shake his hand or slap palms with him. On account of how gross he looked. I offered him a pound instead. We tapped fists and he gave me a knowing smile. Like he wanted me to think I was really hip or something. Like we were both really hip or something. On the level. In the know. It was a ridiculous exchange. Humiliating.

I'd already decided not to tell my mother and just mix the water with ice and put it next to her plate at dinner. I'll build her confidence, I thought. She'd never even know why she wasn't craving a smoke! She'd think she'd quit already! How devious of me! What a ruse! Once she gets past the crucial first couple days, she'll be able to quit all on her own! I was very proud of myself. I kept thinking about it. Patting myself on the back.

Of course, I'd have no control over what kind of water she drank tomorrow when she got to work. I realized that. But whatever. I guess

I thought that maybe if she realized at the end of the night that she hadn't thought once of the mild, satisfying taste of a cigarette since before dinner, maybe she'd be inspired to turn over a new leaf. I could give her one every night for a work week. I was very optimistic. No more death!!!! No more worries!!!! A new dawn!!!! A better life for everyone!!!!

At dinner my sisters knew I was up to something weird. I could tell by the way they were watching me. And looking at each other sideways. It was hard not to laugh. Quite a few times I had to use my napkin to hold back the chuckles. I was being sneaky. It felt good. Kelly wanted to know why I'd taken it upon myself to set the table. My mother told the both of them to hush. I was just being a sweetheart and taking care of her because I knew she had a hard day at work. "Moms deserve to relax sometimes too," I beamed at my sisters. Even though my mother *had* cooked the spaghetti, meat sauce, and garlic bread and mixed up the salad all on her own without me.

But the thing is, my mother was mostly just drinking light beer during dinner. I only saw her take three little sips of her water, but she drank at least two cans of beer. I watched her closely. Her glass was still full when the meal was over. That meant I had to clean up after dinner too, so she wouldn't pour out her water, which cost me like more than five dollars a bottle, plus that ten-dollar tip to the crackhead who scored it for me.

After cleaning up, I positioned the glass next to her in the kitchen while she was making phone calls. She didn't even touch it. She acted like it was a fishbowl or something. She even heated up a cup of coffee left over from this morning. She had another beer. I didn't feel like standing there all night watching a glass of water. I've never had any patience. But I hung around for a while anyway. I missed a rerun of *The Simpsons*, which I watch every night. The news was on in the background while she talked to her sister—and smoked a cigarette—so I picked up on some of that while pretending to look through the refrigerator for an after-dinner snack. A few people had died in the city today in gunfire. One of them was a little boy on training wheels who had ridden his bike through the crossfire of a drug dispute on the west side. Another child was missing in Baltimore County. There was also a story about some kind of cool pet robots that had become popular in Tokyo. But then they did one about breast cancer that was just way too depressing and I had to get out of there. I went outside the garage beneath the deck in back to fuck around on this little PVC grind rail I have. Then I switched the trucks on my skateboard. But mainly I smoked a bowl. Two bowls. And a couple cigarettes.

~

Today was all good. It was hot out and Robby picked me up in his dad's truck and we floated down the Gunpowder on black rubber inner tubes. I kind of remember doing this with my older cousins when I was little, but I don't think I enjoyed it as much back then. You move along pretty slow most of the time. When I was little I guess all I wanted was to go fast and hit rapids. But drifting merrily along was more than fine with me today, just rolling down the icy falls with your tube spinning lazy circles and a six-pack of Boh floating behind you in a plastic bag. The water keeps your beer kind of cold. You hang your head back and stare up at the green foliage that reaches out over the stream. The light dances. A filter for the sun. It makes you feel like the world is upside down when you're lying that way.

The water was cold at first, like dunking your nads in a glass of ice water. But we smoked a blunt and after a while I didn't even notice. Besides it was HOT AS SHIT out this afternoon. Humid. That's why we went tubing in the first place. Duh. And the best thing is that even though it cost us ten dollars to rent the tubes, we stole them afterward and then gave them each custom paint jobs with spray paint from Robby's father's garage, so nobody'll recognize them from now on. We can go wherever we want on the river whenever we want. Like tube fucking pirates! ARRRRRRRGGGGHHHH, BITCH, I say to that. BLOW ME DOWN!

Robby wrote BEASTER BUNNY on the side of his tube of course, and also drew a pot leaf that came out looking like an asterisk. I just wanted to do camouflage on mine so I could blend in with nature, but it was too hard to make the camo look right, especially with the colors we had—lime green and blue and Easter egg yellow. I ended up writing SNIZARD on the side of my tube. I don't know why I did it. It just came to me. I could have written RETARD I guess. But I didn't.

~

I was so psyched on floating down that river yesterday that I tried to convince Robby we should go tubing again today—mostly because I needed his car to get out there, although I wouldn't have minded the company. But he wasn't interested. Anyway he had to be at the animal hospital in Towson, where he works cleaning up dog turds and locking things in cages. So I ended up spending the better part of the afternoon wandering around the neighborhood all by myself like a dummy, pondering the answer to a specific, peculiar question. It felt like some ancient riddle passed down through history by all the great mystics. That is: Do birds fuck?

I'm serious. I mean, they lay eggs, right? Like fish, or snakes that just writhe around and don't really fuck as far as I'm concerned.

Male and female snakes do it kind of like human lesbians, rubbing up against each other and stuff. Seriously. Look it up on the Internet. But can you imagine two bluebirds going at it? I mean, the physics of it just seem way too awkward. Their backward legs, their wings, their shape . . . The whole prospect of bird sex seemed ridiculous to me today. Of course they fuck, you know. But, HOW? I just couldn't wrap my head around that shit. No matter how hard I tried.

It was beautiful out and the sky was practically see-through. So I ended up bumming around all distracted with my head tilted up toward the treetops and phone poles, thinking all these filthy thoughts about nature, when I rounded a corner in Roland Park Northway and bumped square into the bony-chested madras shirt of an old gray man with a red nose. The murderer from across the street. The one that my sisters are so fond of spying on.

He must've been watching the ground in the same way that I was watching the sky. He looked up at me real startled. Not so much from the impact, because we were both going real slow, but from seeing me I guess. Like he'd just bumped into a dinosaur on the way to the mailbox or something. He smelled like cologne and egg sandwiches.

For a split second I thought he was staring at the big-ass purple blotch on my eye, which I guess can be kind of shocking for some people when they first see it. But then when he kept on staring I figured he was just buried down deep in his thoughts the way old people get sometimes. Anyway, if he was looking at my birthmark he didn't act all polite like a sweetheart the way most people do after they realize I've caught them staring. Not this guy. This old bird just snuffled and looked back down at his shoes before taking out a plain white handkerchief and coughing into it.

"It's okay, fella," he said, like he thought I was about to apologize or something. Which I wasn't. Then he winked at me. I think.

It might have been a tic. "It's all right, kid. If you're going anywhere important," he croaked. "You're gonna end up walking on some bodies . . . And mine's as good as any. It's already close enough to the dirt."

He carefully dusted off the front of his shirt with the handkerchief, even though his shirt wasn't noticeably dusty or anything. I stood in the sun with my eyes all chinked up and watched the old man hike off at a worm's pace. He was headed in the direction of the front gate. I tried to imagine where he could possibly be walking to and how long it would probably take him to get there at the speed he was traveling. And for the life of me I couldn't help wondering why he didn't just take his hatchback.

~

I often HATE the way it seems like every time I walk into a room I find the television on. I don't know why I hate it, but I do. On the other hand I can't help watching TV most of the time. Like more of the time than not really. Especially if I'm all by myself. If I can't hear anything in the background of my life—music, static, dialogue, commercials—I feel uncomfortable or something. I think I'm hooked. It's complicated. Sometimes I wish the machine had never been invented, but that doesn't mean I stop watching.

~

When I was little, my butt always stank. No kidding. I wasn't really potty trained, not like consistently, until I was about four years old. After that I didn't wipe so good for a long time either. I was always in too much of a hurry. I usually missed that little indent behind my asshole. The one at the base of your tailbone. It caught feces like a spoon. The smell didn't bother me too much at that age. It was sort of comforting to be honest. But then I started noticing it more. Probably because I started school. I didn't want to smell like that around other people. I began to feel self-conscious. I decided to do something about it. That made me wipe extra hard. Too hard. I got rashes. I carried Gold Bond in my book bag. Baby powder. There were always dingleberries. Now, I try to shower after every time I take a dump. This is a hard habit to keep. I end up taking showers at odd times. At people's houses. Sometimes people ask questions. My hair's always wet. I am always dripping.

~

Got my dad to drop me off at the concrete park in Pigtown this morning when he went to work downtown. I was supposed to meet him outside his building for a ride around five this afternoon. Or I had money for a cab if I got antsy and couldn't wait that long. Pigtown is kind of trashy with a lot of boarded-up houses and meth freaks, but also some families and a shitload of renovations I noticed this morning out the window of my dad's worn-out old Beemer. The reason it's called Pigtown is on account of how they used to slaughter all the meat there in the olden days. It's where all the death houses and butcher shops were. The rowhomes aren't so bad really, but they were traditionally occupied by the broke and desperate I guess because of the way dead things tend to reek. They kill meat somewhere else now I guess. Somewhere outside the city—probably Texas or something. So Pigtown is kind of this abandoned little hamlet near the stadiums. Anyway that's where the skate park is and today I went skating.

Since it was so early, eight thirty when I got there, the park was empty and I had the whole place to myself for a while. Clean off-white waves of smooth concrete. I could go anywhere I wanted. It felt like a dream. Really it did. No one was even there to look at me. Well, a couple of times these little black kids came over and watched me skate through the chain link fence. They kept talking to me, requesting kickflips and shit. It made me nervous. But mostly they just chased each other around the parking lot with sticks and hunks of asphalt. At around eleven thirty a Blazer rolled up and out hopped three dudes about my age. I'd never seen them before. I was pretty beat already and smoking a cigarette on a ledge near the fence. I watched them pull their boards from the trunk. Squinting real hard, I could see the girl in the driver's seat well enough to tell she was hot. Dark hair. Probably like seventeen. Soft purple lips in the shape of a heart. Bangs in the late stages of growing out. Somebody's older sister. I imagined her bent over on top of my Mortal Kombat sheets, ass wriggling like a Jell-O mold. It was a ridiculous fantasy. I hadn't even seen the poor girl's body from the neck down and I was almost hard. My penis is out of control.

She drove off and I ended up skating with these kids for a while in the mini capsule bowls, carving and stalling on the spine transfer in the middle. At first we didn't say anything really, just nodded and stood around watching each other's moves. After a while things warmed up a bit and I learned that the older sister belonged to the smallest boy, who was about my size and had freckles and a lip ring and arched eyebrows like the Joker. His name was Ryan, I think. I sort of missed the other two dudes' names and I was afraid to ask twice so I just ended up calling them "dude" and "man" for the rest of the day. They were from out in Owings Mills. I listened to them talk shit about Ryan's highly fuckable older sister, but I didn't know if it was cool or not to join in the fun. I'd just met them, after all.

After a while the sun started really heating things up. I seriously thought birds were gonna start to fall from the sky. Everyone was pretty worn out and thirsty. Especially me. More and more people kept showing up at the park, older guys, guys on bikes, a whole bunch of people, so we four decided to clear out and skate over toward the inner harbor. Maybe get some food or something. Everyone agreed it would be a good thing if we had herbage. I had some back at home that I'd gotten from the Beaster Bunny, but I didn't say anything about it, just mentioned I could probably find them something later if they wanted. They asked me for my phone number. I gave them my mom's, but I doubted they'd call.

We skated until we could see the stadiums and then we skated past the stadiums and into the harbor. We got chased off the Legg Mason banks by this chubby meter maid. The dudes I was with wanted to skate down Baltimore Street. So we did, but we were all too young to go into any of the strip clubs. Instead we just kind of did powerslides on the sidewalk out front and waited for the callers and doormen to yell at us so we could give them the finger. Then we went into this newsstand and looked at butterfly knives and stash cans and the outside of porno tapes without buying anything. Someone said they wanted to skate the Columbus Statue in Little Italy. So we headed over there, even though every skater in Baltimore knows how busted it is. On the way, we stopped at the aquarium to check out the seals, which are the only animals that are stationed outside and free to the public. Ryan threw a nickel into the seal tank like it was a wishing well. He wished the seals would start fucking. The other boys laughed. One of the seals gave us a friendly look before diving after the coin. I laughed too. But I was secretly worried the seal might choke on the nickel. I wished I could reach in and pick it up without anyone seeing. Then one of the dudes got bored and decided the seals were lame I guess, so we moved on to Little Italy.

We'd hit the statue for like ten minutes until, sure enough, a security guard came by and asked us to leave, which was fine with me because my legs were feeling like rubber and I wasn't landing anything anyway. We rode into Fells Point. The plan was to go look at CD's. We'd skated pretty fucking far already and, like I said, it was hot out. So I took off my T-shirt. I used it to wipe the sweat from my hair. I left it on top of my head. I meant to put the shirt back on before we got to Broadway, but when I looked over my shoulder I noticed the other guys had seen me and done the same thing. Now we were riding down the street shirtless, all four of us, in a line. So here we come, four bare-chested idiots rolling past all these H & S Bakery trucks at full speed with rags draped over our heads like Aunt Jemima. I felt a little embarrassed. Like a big dork. A retard.

We went into this head shop on Eastern Avenue. We had to put our shirts on first. There's a big talking parrot in the back of the store that alerted the boss lady to our presence. She tossed us out right away. We weren't old enough. On the street outside was a dirty homeless. He was hassling people for change. I noticed his sign was double-sided. One side said: LAID OFF + HEP C = NEED A BLESSING. The other side said: HELP A MAN GET A BEER DAMMIT . . . PLEASE! I didn't feel too bad for him. I figured one side must work when the other didn't. Ryan and the dudes thought he was a riot. One of them gave him a dollar. I wouldn't give two loose shits for that shifty old bum, but I did feel slightly apprehensive when I saw this tiny blonde girl like four or six years old lying all alone on the step of an empty storefront across the street. I wondered what she was up to. She reminded me of a fish in a bowl. She was wearing a sad little cotton dress and a pair of Aqua Socks that gave her clown feet. Her face looked sort of doped up to me. I felt bad seeing her.

We headed down Broadway to the Sound Garden and hung out at the listening station but didn't buy anything. Then we decided to eat at the market so we rode back up the street. I had a gyro. After eating, we were all out of ideas. Except me. "Let's get some fishheads," I declared, all happy with myself for being so clever. "And bake them on somebody's dashboard."

We hooked up four rockfish heads from the fishman at the market. I thanked him myself. Then we started trolling up and down the sidewalks with an eye out for car windows that were left open a crack because of the heat. The dudes I was with were practically pissing their pants at the prospect of putting a fishhead in somebody's ride. They were really gung-ho about my prank.

Cracked windows weren't hard to find. But since the drivers were always off somewhere, you had to be patient and wait around if you wanted to see their reaction, which was the whole point I guess. Plus we were too scared to loiter around a car with a bloody fishhead in it. We didn't want to be too suspicious. We probably looked like A-1 pranksters to most regular Joes already. So we dicked around for a while. We went all the way up past the bong store and managed to plant three heads on the way. We planned to look for the owners on the way back down Broadway. I hit the first car—a metallic blue Camry with an interior full of Happy Meal boxes and perfume samples—and the other guys took turns after me. I just kind of hung back and dug the scene mostly from then on. Actually, I thought the whole prank was pretty stupid by this point—I was feeling guilty—but I didn't want to tell the guys that because I was the one who suggested it.

Anyway, as we were walking back down the far side of the street with an eye out for open windows and for the owners to return to the ones we'd already hit, I saw the little blonde girl again. We passed right next to her. She was sitting up now in her little cave off the sidewalk and she was holding something shiny in her lap that I couldn't quite make out, even squinting. I found myself unconsciously moving a step closer to look. Maybe she was holding brass knuckles? Holy shit. She was holding brass knuckles. I blinked twice. Her little baby hands were in her lap, holding a pair of genuine knuckle-dusters. She was playing with them. Catching the sun against the brass, transfixed by the glare.

Like I said, I was pretty exhausted from skating. I thought I might be seeing things. All at once I wondered who her parents were and why they'd abandoned her. But more than that I couldn't figure out why anyone would give a baby girl brass knuckles. To defend herself? It seemed pretty ludicrous. What would she do with them? It was almost more likely that she came from another planet or something. Especially the way she seemed so calm and natural sitting there, like she'd just crawled out of a crack in the sidewalk. I watched her in freeze-frame. She didn't notice me. I started to make up all these little, like, stories about her. All at once. Nobody else seemed to notice the girl. Or they didn't acknowledge her if they did. I couldn't understand it. I looked around, but people were just moving along, minding their own business. Loud salsa music was playing outside the Puerto Rican grocery. Someone was selling bootleg DVD's. A construction worker was waiting for change outside a snowball stand . . . I wanted to help this girl. Get her a snowball at least. Then BAM! like that, this big black woman in a tank top with meat hanging off her bones popped out of the vacant storefront and scooped the child up. She took the brass knuckles from the little girl's hands. That's when I realized they were not brass knuckles at all. Just a shiny trinket on a sort of heavy-looking key ring.

Seeing me standing there like a dunce, the fat woman shot me a dirty look. She tried to shield the girl between her big breasts. I'd freaked her out. She thought I meant the child harm. I looked down at my feet and realized for the first time how close I had gotten to this kid. I could have touched her. I felt like I'd just emerged from a coma. I tried to look around for Ryan and his boys, but I couldn't find them anywhere in the pedestrian traffic. I went to the curb and stood on my skateboard to get a better view. They were gone. I was all alone. I turned back and saw the fat woman running across the street, the little girl's head bobbing up and down over her shoulder. The little girl was watching me. A huge grin split the baby fat on her face. She waved at me with her whole arm. I waved back.

Then my stomach started to shrink. I saw where they were headed. Straight for the metallic blue Camry. The one I'd put a fishhead inside. It was baking on the front seat with all the perfume samples. I could picture it. Beady-eyed and stinking. I skated off before I could see their reaction. I imagined the little girl's tears and felt bad. I almost told my dad about it on the way home that evening, but I didn't.

~

Sometimes when I say something by accident or whatever and my mother's face crumples up like a paper bag and I know she's about to cry, I feel all low and nasty like I owe all my time as long as we're both still alive to loving her and protecting her and making her happy and comfortable for the rest of her days. Other times I feel like she needs a poke in the eye. And I want to give it to her. Should god hate me for that?

~

News on the march! There's a family of moles living in this mound of dirt behind one of the manicured firs in my mother's development. I first found them while playing Hide and Go Seek Tag with my sisters and all the little neighborhood brats, using the gate and the vine-covered chain link fence around the development as our boundaries and the big oak in the center as base. I was hiding by myself, sitting on my butt in the dirt smoking one of my mom's cigarettes when all the moles began popping out of these baby-sized openings in the earth near my legs. They moved low to the ground, slipping into each little bellybutton in the mound's surface. Without noticing me, I think. They weren't scared of me at least. I could've picked one up and put it in my pocket if I'd wanted to. But for some reason I didn't. I just watched them. It made me feel like a giant sitting there with these all these tiny animals scurrying around my legs. It was nice. Aren't moles supposed to be blind? I couldn't be sure from looking at them, but their eyes were very small if they existed at all. The little guys were actually kind of cute. They looked like worms. Mammals, but worms.

~

Okay, so this spring word got out at like every school in the north Baltimore area about this number you could call if you wanted to get cussed out by this old lady. "The Crazy Lady" is what people called her. Like there was only one in the world. It's not that much different than "Retard" if you think about it. Anyway, I first called her number with David Frimke whose older sister was a sophomore at RPCS and had been calling the number with her friends during free periods.

But really everyone was doing it. Nobody knew who discovered the number. It was just everywhere all of a sudden, all at once.

The voice on the other end of the line sounded like a cartoon to me. A cartoon that smoked too many cigarettes. She reminded me of the evil stepmother in Snow White when she transforms herself into an old woman with a wart on her nose, which is pretty weird because no one ever actually *saw* the Crazy Lady. She could've been like thirty years old. Or twenty. Or beautiful. She could have been anyone for all I know. There's a lot of people around Baltimore with fucked-up sounding voices, not just her. Besides her gravelly voice, she had a real dirty mouth. But from listening to her you could tell she didn't have Tourette's or anything. She was just plain bonkers.

"LICK MY PUSSYFARTS YOU CUNTBAG SKUNKFUCKING PERVERT! YOU GOAT! YOU PIG!" That was the kind of shit she'd tell you. And you could cuss her back if you wanted or ask her questions or put her on speakerphone at a birthday party. Or just sit there and pass the phone back and forth with your friends or whatever . . . People just loved this phone number. It was a total hit. I know some people who called like ten times a day. A lot of the time when you called during peak hours, like at lunchtime or right after school, the line would be busy. You'd have to sit there and press redial over and over until you got through. Like a radio contest. People would do conference calls. "I SHIT ON YOUR DEAD FACE! DIE, DIE, DIE, YOU EVIL SHITLOVER! WHORE! SLUT! NIGGER! YOU EAT DOGGY TURDS! YOU DRINK CUM!" She loved to talk about death. It was gnarly. I told the kids I was going to school with over in Hamilton about her. They thought it was gnarly. They started calling her too.

But I kinda felt bad for her in all of this springtime insanity. The poor woman obviously lived all by herself. Her phone was ring-ing off the hook at all hours of the day. Couldn't her neighbors hear it? Did nobody know what was happening? Sometimes it made me uncomfortable talking to her. She scared me. Like a witch. And what if she was somebody's grandmother? I felt bad. But I kept calling all the time I guess because everybody else around me was doing it. Anyway it *was* pretty fucking funny sometimes. My little sisters thought she was hilarious. They knew about her before I did, in fact.

I even called her by myself a few times, nicely, hoping I could maybe reason with her. It was corny as hell. I admit it. (Admit it? To a fucking journal? Is this really lame? Am *I* lame?) But I called her anyway. And she cussed me out. What's your name, I'd ask her. Or, do you have any relatives I could call that might want to help you? Or even just, do you want to be my friend? You know, talk to her. Shit like that. But she just swore at me every time. "I KILLED YOUR MOTHER EVERY DAY FOR A YEAR, ASSHOLE! AND SHE FUCKING LOVED IT! SHE SQUIRMED!!!"

The Crazy Lady was too far gone to be helped, I guess. Or she didn't trust me. Eventually—after like two and a half months almost—her phone was disconnected. When you called you'd just get some robot voice telling you no service. I remember hoping that maybe her son had come to visit her and saw what was happening to his ol' mom and the conditions she was living under and whisked her away to some place in the country where he could visit her often and they could feed her good drugs and make her feel happy and comfortable for the rest of her days. I hoped that, but I couldn't help thinking that maybe she had passed away all by herself in her wasted apartment. Some superintendent probably discovered her corpse and had the telephone line disconnected. I couldn't help worrying that she had died and spent the last two and a half months of her life answering the telephone and cussing into the speaker. And that no one would ever even know about it.

~

My uncle Rick told me the cicadas are coming back this summer. He seemed excited about it. I told him I wasn't even born yet the last time they came. "You ain't seventeen yet?" he asked, even though he obviously must know I'm not seventeen. I look twelve. I told him my age. "*Whew,*" he said. "Fourteen. That *is* young. You're gonna go out one of these nights, get loose, and wake up my age. And the cicadas will be coming back again. It happens to the best of us . . . Boy, Miles. Time sure does fly."

I couldn't help thinking, fly where?

~

I'm hanging out on the sidewalk in front of my mother's, practicing my shuv-its off the curb, when this black chick pulls up in her car. The same black chick I saw with the old dude before, the Killer. She watches me for a second and I guess I feel the need to impress her, which is how I always feel for some reason when I catch people watching me skate. I pop a big one and she claps. I like her smile. Her teeth look so white, like a genuine African's, straight out of *National Geographic*. So I get cocky. I try to bust out a tre flip, hoping she'll dig it. I land on my tail, bust my ass on the edge of the curb. She claps again, this time bent over cackling, then waddles all wobbly up the walkway, shaking her bubble butt into the old man's front door. She has her own key, I notice. I wonder if she's cleaning the place. Nah, I think, her nails are too long for that.

~

Besides biting my nails until they got infected and green pus would come out, when I was little I was also quite fond of picking my nose. REALLY picking it. Like so it would get all lined with crunchy scabs and dark blood. Then I would pick at the scabbage. And it would bleed more. Fresh. And get infected. It hurt real bad and was pretty embarrassing, but I couldn't help myself. I was obsessed. If I could feel a little piece of something up there, anything at all, I was going for it. I was a perfectionist in that way. I felt like I couldn't breathe all the time. I needed better ventilation, so I picked.

It's a lot better now. I mean, I still do pick it sometimes but no more than anyone else probably. At least I hope not. I can't remember the last time I had scabby boogers. The only nose bleeds I've gotten lately have been from fistfights and snorting Ritalin. So life is a lot better now, I suppose.

~

I absolutely HATE the dentist. To whom it may concern, Miles Lover hates the fucking dentist. You will never catch me in another dentist's chair as long as I live. I swear to Christ. I DON'T CARE if my teeth fall out. I *want* fucking dentures. Seriously. No brushing. Just stick them in a cup at night and sleep easy. Fuck the dentist.

It's not that I'm some kind of pussy either. I like to think I have a pretty high threshold for pain. I was always decent at playing Mercy and I wreck all comers in Bloody Knuckles. Plus we used to play this game in our elementary school bathroom where you'd put a toothpick in your mouth horizontal so the two points were held in place by the fleshy tissue inside your cheeks. Then you'd stand next to the wall.

Your friends would take turns tap-tap-tapping you harder and harder on the side of your face so the toothpick would keep stabbing the inside of your mouth. You're supposed to take it as long as you can before calling uncle. The one who can take the pain longest is the proud winner. I could let my classmates do this to me for the longest time. Sometimes it would freak everybody out. Really, it would. They'd get all excited. I liked the way their faces looked when they watched. All grossed out, but also kind of impressed. Pumped. That would numb things a little . . . For as long as I can remember I've been hearing a story about some kid who put a hole through his cheek doing this. I'm not sure if it's true or not, but it could definitely happen. Anyway, none of that compares to the dentist's office. Sharp, toothy pain. Fuck that. I can't handle the fucking dentist.

When I was a kid, me and my sisters had this Jewish guy for a dentist. His daughter was in my class and he had puzzles and stuffed animals and a mini plastic ball pit in the corner of his waiting room. I despised him. I would bite his fingers. Later on, I went to this Jamaican dude, but he wasn't a Rasta or anything. I always wondered how a boy from Kingston, Jamaica, could grow up to be a dentist in Towson, Maryland of all places. But I never got around to asking him. His hands were always in my mouth. I couldn't enunciate. Anyway, I just switched dentists again because of a change in my mother's insurance or something like that, which I don't fully understand. So now it's an Asian lady with freckles and a big torture-movie smile full of shiny teeth. I went to see her this morning.

Originally the plan was to get my teeth cleaned and go home. My mom dropped me off. She was going to run a few errands and look at something on the Internet for her work and then come back to get me. Did I mention I hate the dentist? First of all, the most foreboding odor in the entire world is that weird fluoride filling gel flavored-toothpaste nitrous oxide smell you get when you enter the waiting room. It's impossible for me to separate that odor from the sound of the drill in my head.

There were framed posters of chimpanzees all over the walls in this chick's waiting room. And this weird lighting that reminded me of an alien autopsy. I passed the time reading a pamphlet about flossing technique until my name was called.

She started out by asking me some irrelevant questions about what grade I'm in and what my favorite class is and do I play any sports and all that. She gave me about two seconds to answer before shoving her fingers in my mouth. You'd think there was a golden egg lodged in my throat! Fine with me, get it over with. She poked around with this fishhook thing that looked pretty nasty, but wasn't too uncomfortable. Except she kept talking under her breath as she did it, counting on her fingers in Chinese or something. It made me nervous. I already felt like I was going to vomit. I had felt this way ever since I woke up this morning and I was reminded of the appointment.

Then she moved onto the sonic cleaning. That kind of hurt. And I hate the noise it makes. It sounds too much like the drill. "*Sensitive,*" she kept whispering, as if I didn't already know. "*Leetle beet sensitive.*" She held her fingers real close together to show me much it should hurt. Leetle beet.

Turns out I had five cavities. Two of them were really big. I had no idea. But she found them right off. All right, I figured, I'm done for the day. I can go smoke pot, come back in like two weeks or whatever and get those bitches filled up. But seriously, I was ready to go home at this point. I was tired and like I said, I hate the dentist.

But instead of asking *me*, like anybody would be interested in *my* plan of action for *my* fucking mouth, Dr. Khan—something like that—called out to my mother, who I guess had come back and was outside waiting. Together they chose to fill my teeth today. That would be most convenient for everyone, they decided. The doctor sounded delighted about the procedure. Mom too. I might as well have been a patient at the veterinarian's office, for all my say in the matter.

Dr. Khan told me I looked tough enough and she thought I could forego the Novocaine. She was buttering me up. I could tell. She actually called me a "big boy" when she suggested it. Then she told me that it would only take longer if I got the Novocaine and *then* she finally asked if I wanted any. I got the feeling she wanted me to say "No." I did. I hate the stuff anyway. I always chew holes in my cheeks and my lip when I get it. Besides, I just wanted to get out of there. She began to stuff me full of cotton. And then she started drilling.

The drill is the loudest thing in the universe when it's inside your face. High-pitched speed metal . . . *SSSSSZZZZZZZSSSZZZZSSSTTT*. . . Even on the three cavities that were supposed to be shallow . . . It fucking killed me. One was on the back of my front tooth. There was a moment when I thought she might push the drill straight through. The burning smell is the worst. Smoke, tooth decay grinding away, tiny nerves frying. She kept showing me little pieces of decay in the palm of her latex glove. They looked like tiny fossils. I kept my hands in my pockets. I broke like six cigarettes, squeezing my pack. With my other hand I squeezed a disposable lighter. I tried to concentrate on Dr. Khan's freckles. They were enormous! I was being sucked into one of them. I thought I was going to swallow my tongue. I couldn't control my saliva. Dr. Khan was screeching at me continuously. She sounded like a pterodactyl. "Keep mouth open! Open mouth! Bigger! No move tongue or things get wet! Wet no good! Mouth open or I drill again!"

Every muscle in my body tightened. My brain throbbed. My toes curled up inside my skate shoes. I couldn't keep my legs in the chair. My feet kept rising on their own. I couldn't control them. The drill is the pits.

The last two fillings were the worst. By far. I pinched my eyelids shut and tried to convince myself I could convert the pain into pleasure. I imagined it might be possible to achieve complete body control like some gnarly kung fu master. I'd learn to love the pain. After all, I thought, it's only a sensation of the body, just like any other. It didn't work. The pain hurt. The cold water she was rinsing the holes with rocked my nerve endings. The air she used to dry the holes tickled them. It hurt like shit. I had to resist the urge to get up and flee. I used to sometimes jump out of the barber's chair during haircuts when I was a kid. I almost did that today.

I was pretty shocked at the size of the holes she dug out. I could fit the entire tip of my tongue in one of them. She filled the cavities with this crusty cement stuff. It tasted like exhaust. I wasn't supposed to eat, drink, or smoke cigarettes for at least eight hours. I ended up doing all three after my mom went back to work. Plus bong hits. When Dr. Khan led me out of the waiting room my knees felt weak, like I'd been on a boat all day. I leaned against the wall. My mom looked at me with a big smile and asked, "How was it?"

On the ride home my mom stopped at Cimino's to buy cigarettes and a lotto ticket. Afterward we passed this dopey little old folks' home on Melrose. It reminds me of a crummy motel, with outdoor hallways carpeted in Astroturf. It's kind of a depressing place to look at. One of those real small places, the kind where I always imagine old people rotting away unattended, shitting themselves and stuff. Like I said, depressing. My grandmother lives in an old folks' home out in Owings Mills, but hers is a lot bigger and nicer looking, almost like a college campus or something.

Anyway, as we passed by the short white building—it's only two stories tall—there was this silver-haired couple walking along the side of the road. My head was throbbing from the dentist and the sun was sort of in my eyes, but I couldn't help being interested in them anyway. I squinted through my mother's windshield. They were old and shrunken, but they were holding hands and looked well at ease. The way they had their heads tilted up, you could tell they were enjoying the sun. I usually feel guilty or sad around old people. I don't like them. They remind me of things I don't want to think about. But watching this cool old couple, I felt happy and sort of free, like I was caught up in some big gust of wind, like everybody was. I watched a private ambulance drift silently out of the parking lot, looking like it had nowhere to go. Somehow that was beautiful. But I didn't tell my mother. I kept it for myself.

~

The truth is, I have a terrible memory. I put my hands over my eyes to try to remember things I want to put in my journal, but my head feels like a cantaloupe . . . organic, rotting away.

Except, when I go to squeeze it, my skull is hard as rock.

The stuff in my journal sounds fake when I go to reread it. So I don't do that anymore.

~

Strangest thing earlier. I was just kind of skating around Roland Park Northway with my slingshot and maybe an eye out for birds. It's hard to hit a bird with a slingshot. I usually just miss them by a smidgeon. Today I found a bird's nest in a Christmas tree covered with small violet berries. There weren't any birds in it, but there were three pale blue eggs. They were small, but bright. Easy to spot. I didn't even have to get that close. I heard that if a mama bird knows you've been near its nest then it'll orphan its eggs. I felt shitty about that. So I stayed about ten feet away and just watched it, no touching.

Then Miss Sandy Diamond came powerwalking past me, all MILF'd out in these stretch pants and a sweatshirt cropped over her shoulders at the neck and high across the belly *Flashdance*-style. She was wearing her iPod and a heart monitor, but even with all those distractions, she noticed me and waved. I could feel the red hot grin spreading across my face. There was nothing I could do about it. I just waved back, so fast it's not even funny. My forearm was flapping away like a hummingbird's wing.

I already had an erection. Miss Sandy Diamond always gives me boners when she's jogging. I usually run home and work my groin like a bicycle pump. It's exhausting. I'm covered in sweat. The tip of my penis stings. I come back out with dark rings under my eyes. Well, today was no different. I watched her Spandexed thighs slide back and forth against each other until she disappeared around the bend, then I tucked my hard-on in the elastic of my boxer shorts—a trick I learned in Nam—and started pushing off toward home.

That's when I heard it. This crazy music sprinkling from the trees and over the houses, out of chimneys and up through the ground. Banjo music, I think. All around me. It was soft and eerie and clear as day, rolling out fast like spring water. Or quicksilver. I thought I was imagining it. Me and my boner pushed and pushed through this shower of music until I was at my mother's front door. I shouldered it and ran upstairs. When I got into the bathroom, I sat down on the toilet and started pulling my dick. It was quiet in there except for the hiss of running pipes. I tried to open the window to hear if the music was still going on outside. But it's awkward unwinding the bathroom window from the shitter in my mother's condo. In the corner where the toilet is, there isn't enough space for your elbow to move. I had to concentrate. By the time I got the damn thing open, my erection was gone. But the music was still playing. So I just sat there. And listened.

~

The other day I was with my sisters and Ashley Vidal at the pool and Ashley asked me a question. "Why do you always have so many scabs on your elbows and knees from skateboarding?" She actually asked it just like that. For real. Answered her own question.

"I shred," I told her. "And when you're really shredding, you fall. And when you fall, you get mutilated."

"Oh," she said, and left her mouth hanging open like she was trying to understand.

"Scabs are cool," I told her. "That's why."

~

When I'm by myself sometimes, I make noises. LOUD noises. And dance. I can't help it. Like if I walk into a house I know is empty I might scream cuss words or nonsense at the top of my lungs. Or if I'm securely locked in my room late at night I might sing a little melody in tongues as I flip through a magazine. I suspect other people do the same thing. I watch for this type of behavior on the reality shows for instance, but I'm always disappointed. I remember people around me, other kids, making weird noises when I was little. More openly. They just do it in private now, I figure. But how can I tell without asking? And if you ask people about the noises they make, they are likely to lie.

I also like to turn up the stereo and dance around my bedroom, especially when I'm high. I'm not a very good dancer. I'm best when I am alone. And high . . . And sometimes when I'm all by myself at home, I get scared. For no reason at all. It's stupid. I'll hear something or just get a weird feeling and go around my house with a big knife or a field hockey stick, checking under beds and stuff. Looking for bad guys . . . Plus I can't keep my hands off my Johnson when I'm watching television. Even when it's soft. My hand just goes down there on its own, without me noticing. I think I like the warmth.

Anyway, moral of the story is that I may not be that much of a weirdo in public, but that doesn't mean I'm not a weirdo. You too. Everyone makes their own noises. Or makes out with their pillowcase. Or swings their ding-dong in circles. They do something strange in private. We're all secret weirdos. In secret. But you can't ever know about anyone else's secret weirdness without spying on them is all. It's like trying to hear a tree in the forest from a downtown intersection.

Maybe that's what the journal is for. Screaming nonsense when you're all alone . . . Howling at the moon when you know it's not looking.

~

A lot of the time I feel ashamed for making a fool of myself. Other times it's not so bad and I say fuck it. I tend to look foolish a lot.

Lately I've been thinking that it's wrong to look down on yourself for being foolish. It leads to looking down on other fools.

Besides, who's got the time to be mortified?

~

What do you want to be when you grow up? Huh? Truth is I don't want to be anything when I grow up. Really. Nothing. Now I know I might be pretty naive, especially about money and shit, and especially because I never really had any loot of my own except my allowance, which gets handed out pretty liberally when I ask for it. But it seems to me that a lot of people's lives start to suck when they decide they want to BE something. They get stuck. It's like they BECOME their job. From then on, all of their time is for sale. Just so they can feel comfortable. It doesn't sound like a very good deal to me. A person's time on earth is not the best bargaining chip, in my opinion. Mostly because you can't replace it. But also because you never know how much you've got left.

~

One of the main reasons I used to get in so much trouble at school was that I couldn't keep my mouth shut. All the time I would say these things . . . that came into my head . . . even when I knew they'd get me in trouble. Even if I didn't mean what I was saying. I'd mainly make jokes or comments that I was just dying to see somebody else make. I'd almost always rather one of my classmates made the joke instead of me. Then I'd get to listen. And laugh. You can't laugh at your own jokes. But either the kids in my class wouldn't think up the same joke or they were too smart to actually say it out loud if they had.

Example: There was this teacher I had called Mister D. Old Mister D was kind of a pompous dude, but pretty smart I guess and sometimes kind of funny. He had a beard and wore fuzzy neckties and corduroy jackets. Anyway, he was very sarcastic and he was all the time making jokes at the expense of his students. Most of the kids thought it was funny. Well, this one time Mister D made a wisecrack about this boy in my class named Greg Chodak. Chodak was kind of a smelly kid. His hair was always caked together like he hadn't washed it in a while.

Mister D made a joke about Chodak's mother bathing him in the Jones Falls. I couldn't help saying something, even though I wanted to hear Chodak do it himself. I would have preferred to hear it out of his mouth. Or any mouth besides mine.

“That's not so bad,” I found myself saying, loud enough for the whole lab to hear me. “All I ever do when I'm feeling dirty is dump a glass of ice water on my crotch.” I got sent to the Black Chair for that one. Then the headmaster made me talk to the school psychiatrist.

~

Big news! Last night I snuck out with Gary. We went to U.B. Fields with all these St. Paul's girls. Well, we didn't actually *sneak out* because my dad wasn't even home and he wouldn't have given a fuck anyway. But the girls snuck out. And we met them. We took a cab. We sat in the back seat outside Open Sundays while the driver went in to get us beer. The cabbie was this fat Russian dude named Stan. “Shtaann,” is how he says it. It's funny to hear him talk.

Supposedly Stan had done this for Gary a few times already this summer. Gary had his business card. Stan gave me the card, too. Pretty cool, right?

When we got to the fields with our thirty-pack, the girls weren't there yet. We drank beer and waited. I smoked a cigarette. Gary packed a dip. We lit off a couple M-80s. Then the ladies showed up.

You could hear them first, through the bushes. They were still on the trail. They sounded high-pitched and far-off, like fairies. Or chickens . . . The field lights made everything look weird. Like the sun was about to come up. And the electricity made a buzzing noise like flies hovering over a turd.

The girls had brought a box of wine with them and a fifth of some broke-ass vodka called Boris. We all started to get pretty drunk. Tyler Sommerly was with them. He's in the grade above us at B.L. He must have driven. Someone else brought playing cards. We sat in a circle and played Fuck the Dealer. I didn't understand the rules really, but I pretended to as best I could. I was glad when the others got bored of playing.

Gary had been sort of working Kari Dunham I guess and after a while I looked around and noticed they were gone. I wanted to hook up with Samantha Maddux, but she was playing aloof. Too pretty, I guess. Fuck her. I ended up making out with her friend Amy, who is slightly chubby but with a cute Irish-looking face that reminds me of Princess Leia. I told her I wanted to get a motorcycle license instead of a regular one, except I was worried about having a place to put my skateboard. She laughed, even though I was being serious. Then she took my hand and led me into the woods.

First thing I remember her saying is she got right up close to my ear and told me she thought I was cute. She actually said that. And like an idiot, I asked without thinking, "What about my spot?"

"I think it's sexy," she whispered.

"Really?" IDIOT! RETARD!

"Yes, really. Where'd you get it?"

"Some Viet hooker splashed me in the face with a glass of burning sherry," I told her. "It happened in Nam."

I don't think she got that I was joking at first. Then she said, "Really?" and I was sure that she didn't get that I was joking.

"No," I told her. "Not really."

After a brief moment of awkwardness, we started kissing again.

I had barely got one of her boobs out when she began to massage my crotch with the heel of her palm. Then she started to take it out. We sat down on her sweatshirt and kissed for a while as she jerked me off. There were dead leaves on the ground all around us. They made a crinkling noise. It was nice, except she had rings on and they kept pinching me. But I didn't say anything. Then she started to go down. At first it was basically like I thought it would be. Only better. Wetter. And more realistic. But there was also an occasional brush of the teeth, which I'd never seen happen in porno. I didn't know what to do with my hands either, so after squeezing her tits a little, I just put them on top of her head. It was dark in the woods. I sometimes thought I could hear animals noises mixed in with the sound of her sucking.

Don't get me wrong. It was awesome. I could scarcely believe this was finally happening to me. But the truth is I felt kind of bad about it too. I brushed her hair back whenever she lifted her head up to rewet her mouth. I'd look at her face and her lips would be all puffy. But then she'd go back down. I mumbled words of encouragement. Corny stuff like, "Mmmm, yeah. You're good at that," or "That's real swell, baby. Keep going," or even just "Thank you." It did feel swell though. So swell in fact that I couldn't help kind of working my dick around in there. Sort of humping her face. Controlling the way she moved her head with my hands. I felt bad about that. I was scared I'd make her puke. Or hurt her throat. But she was fine. It just felt too good to keep still is all. I tried to control myself.

Eventually she got tired and gave up. I wasn't going to come I guess. I felt bad about that too. I felt bad about everything. We kissed a few times, gently, because her lips looked sensitive. Her tongue was all warm when I kissed her. It was weird.

Then Amy took me by the hand again. We walked back to the field and sat down with the others in a circle behind the crease and we sort of cuddled while Tyler told a bunch of dead baby jokes. Eventually he started kind of fucking with me. He kept telling me he thought my little sisters were hot. "Just wait 'til they're in high school," he kept saying. I just kind of fake chuckled and shrugged it off. Amy looked sort of pretty under the lights, in a plain sort of way. But I didn't feel like kissing her again.

The beers had gotten warm, but I drank two anyway. I was drunk. Gary had already called Stan for a ride. He was on his way. Gary and Kari were apparently fighting. We headed up the trail to wait for the cab. I managed to steal the ass-end of the Boris before leaving.

On the ride home we swilled vodka and talked loudly. Stan was in a good mood. He was rocking out to some really loud ethnic music, full of howling and chanting and finger cymbals. It sounded like a carnival or something. Me and Gary kind of got down to it also. I was headbanging and stuff. Stan asked me to roll the bottle under the seat so he could have a sip. I slid the bottle up and he drank from it. I told him how I stole the bottle from the girls. He laughed. He asked how we'd done with our lady friends—"Haf any pussy you've gotten?"

Gary announced that he five-carded his chick. He demonstrated this by cramming all of his fingers into the coin slot on the bulletproof divider. He tried to wiggle them. It was a tight squeeze.

How about me, Stan wanted to know.

"Maybe I got some pussy," I told them. "But it was dark out. And I was in the woods. So maybe not . . . Do most pussies hiss when you fuck them?"

Everyone broke out laughing. Me too. But especially Stan. I thought he was going to crash into the old cemetery next to South Homeland Mews. He almost did. It was scary. I patted myself on the back for making a funny, but I ended up keeping mum on the subject of my blow job. Until now. In the journal. Which doesn't really count, does it?

~

Ever since I first heard the expression, I have always wanted to "Cheat Death." But I don't really like the word "cheat" too much. It implies some form of trickery. When basically all I want to do is rob his ass. "Break yourself, Death," I'd bark. "Empty your fuckin' pockets."

~

I got yelled at yesterday by my mother when Miss Sandy Diamond called to talk to her about an incident involving me and her son Donald earlier in the afternoon. Donald had come by for some reason or other. Mostly to pick up stuff in my bedroom and ask me questions about it. At least that's what it seemed like to me.

Anyway, he was looking at this needlepoint ghost my mother gave me my first Halloween. Halloween is my favorite holiday. It's also my birthday. So this was my first birthday present that Donald was holding. Now, I don't believe in putting sentimental value on my toys or anything, but he was picking at it. So I shot him in the foot with a BB gun. It was only a little spring-load pistol. And he was wearing sneakers. But it scared him, I guess. I shot at the wall next to him, too. The shot bounced off and came back to me. I nearly caught it.

So Donald snitched on me and the outrageously hot Miss Sandy Diamond called my mother to talk. They're new friends, my mom and Miss Sandy. They're both divorced. They both enjoy light beer and red wine and coffee. They both love to talk.

My mom never punishes me. I've seriously never been grounded. By my father either. They've told me I was grounded, but it never sticks. We just yell at each other a lot and my mom goes crazy and I storm outside. It's what comes natural to us. And it works okay, I guess. Miss Sandy, who used to be a family counselor, also happened to suggest that my mother not punish me for shooting her son in the foot. She said she thought I should come over instead and talk to Donald and shake his hand, apologize for shooting him, and then we could be friends. Miss Sandy would make a snack for me and Donald to munch on during our conversation. She said that I might need therapy.

Me and Mom yelled at each other a lot about this. My mom wanted me to go over there for her sake and the sake of her new friendship with Miss Sandy Diamond. She said I was out of control. That I made bad decisions. That I never think about the future. I louse everything up. Couldn't I think of someone else for once?

I yelled back. I said I thought about the future all the time. Constantly I think about it, I said. And about her too. Never myself. Then I grabbed my bike and rode over to the old house on Charles. I smoked two joints there and spent the night. I watched the contractors' mini black-and-white TV. I got a banged-up old skateboard from the garage and rode it on the hardwood floor for fun, doing manuals down the long hallway. I slept beneath an oilcloth. When I came home this morning, my mom was at work. I microwaved popcorn and watched cable until she was due to get back. Then I split for my dad's.

~

Secret: I used to masturbate into my socks. Even after I'd been skateboarding in them and they were really gross. I only stopped doing it after my mom started asking questions. Then I became more careful. I use tissue paper now.

One time the Beaster Bunny told me that he would sometimes jerk off in an old glass of water that had gone stale by his bed. Then he would pour his load out in the toilet.

I asked him if he used the same glass every time or if he used a disposable Styrofoam cup.

"Um, neither," he told me. He looked confused about the question. And from then on it was only cans of grape soda at Robby's house for yours truly, Retard . . .

~

Back when my mom and my dad were still living together most of the time, my manners were constantly being called into question. There was always something wrong with the TONE OF MY VOICE. Everything I said was supposedly rude. Especially toward my mother, who's a nervous woman that talks in jags when she's nervous and she's always nervous so . . . She will endlessly voice the obvious if no one interrupts her. My father would rain temper tantrums upon me whenever I pointed this out. He had his own way of dealing with Mom's constant chatter and instructions. He would make small grunting noises and look down at one of his documents. He always had a stack of documents lying around. I think they were props. His grunting sounded like a bear. Its meaning was obvious. Grunting meant, "Fuck off." But that wasn't considered rude for some reason. Or at least nobody got on his case about it. They were too scared . . .

I spent most of my time outside as usual. Or up in my room. Apparently I couldn't help being rude, or at least sounding that way to my parents, so I just kept to myself. I called them the Tone Police. I was afraid to say anything . . . But occasionally they'd think something I said was funny and they'd tell me about it. Express enjoyment. This confused me. I had to walk a tightrope. The whole fucking house was made of eggshells.

I hated watching the fights that broke out when my folks detected rudeness in my voice. Especially because I didn't usually mean to be rude. It was as if I had committed the ultimate sin. Use of a Less Than Charming Tone. My dad would threaten to kick me out of the house. Or he would refuse to pay my tuition. I'd tell him not to bother. Fuck school, right? He'd call me names. Chase me around the house. My mother would get scared of my father's temper and go to defend me. "Why do you always defend him?" my father would snap. Then they'd start fighting. Something would get broken. My little sisters would cry. Someone would inevitably declare that they were moving out. Maybe the neighbors would call to see if everything was all right. Someone would assure them it was. My dad would tear off in his BMW to go look at a battlefield or something. He was obsessed with ruined forts and places of war and he was always visiting them. Or something.

Now I'm staying at my father's house, because of the fight with my mom. I don't like fighting with her. I don't like fighting with my parents at all, but it's worse with her than my dad. I can laugh at him when I'm alone afterward. He's a buffoon. But sometimes my mother will cry. It hurts my chest to see her like that. She'll get very sad. For days. She really takes things to heart. You can see it in her physical appearance. She'll look older. And pale. Like a washcloth left out to dry. It makes me feel bad to see that. I imagine that's maybe what it feels like when you find out that by accident somehow, you killed somebody . . .

My father hasn't been home for dinner yet this week. I don't mind. I microwave French bread pizzas and eat them out on the deck. I watch crows circling above the earth movers parked in the back lot. They cut in and out of each other in a violent way, but without touching. Against the pink sunlight, they look almost like large, low-flying bats.

~

Summer is sooooo boring. I want to go to the beach. Or maybe not. Maybe I want a job. Robby once said he could get me some work with him at the animal hospital, but I would need a work permit with a guardian's signature, and I would only be able to work so many hours a week. Animals are all right, but what would I spend my new money on? Besides herb, I mean . . .

LIST OF THINGS TO DO WITH MONEY, IF EVER I SHOULD GET SOME:

Buy an island. Or a mountain.

Buy a boat. Or a truck. Buy both.

Buy a chainsaw to clear land.

Build a house. A castle.

Buy gun for hunting.

Buy more guns, for protection.

Build a fence. A big one.

Two pools: one empty, one full.

Hot tub.

Invite girls. Mail-order brides.

Big TVs. A movie theater.

A greenhouse. Seeds. Camouflage.
Security system with cameras like *Scarface.*
Armed guards. Snipers.
A cavalry. Air force. More boats. A whole fleet.
Go nuclear.
Invite more girls.
Invite Mom.

~

Today I met the Killer. Well, I met him before, but today I actually *met* the Killer. His name is Mister Reese.

I woke up early and after a pipe I set off to my mother's, carrying an empty knapsack. I was going to collect some comics and things to take back to my dad's since I figured I'd be staying there for a while. I knew Mom ought to have left for work already, but now that I think about it I wonder if I went over in the morning because I secretly hoped that she would be running late and I might bump into her. Either way, it turned out she was. Running late. Her car was still there. I stood on the welcome mat for nearly a minute without putting my hand on the doorknob. When I finally touched the knob it was warm from the sun. My palm was sweating. I felt bad for whatever I'd done I guess. But at the same time, for some reason, walking through the front door struck me as being a pretty weak thing to do. I pictured her sitting at the kitchen counter in her PJ's, mulling over her coffee and cigarette, watching *Good Morning America* all by herself. Her face would light up when she saw me. She'd reach out for a hug. I'd squeeze her sheepishly and everything would be peachy again. Then she'd ask me nicely to apologize to the Diamonds and the fighting would start all over again. She'd lose control of her breath. Maybe start crying. That would rile me up. I'd say something mean and take off. She'd weep in the car before she left and then pretend she was invincible for the rest of the day while she tried to manage the office at work. I decided to climb up the back of the house and go in through my window instead.

I've always been adept at climbing things. When I would be picked last for touch football at recess I would always tell myself I could climb a tree higher and faster than anyone else in school. Too bad they never picked teams for that. Anyway, getting up to the deck in back is an easy reach from a set of wooden steps that runs alongside our rowhome. These staircases run all throughout the development. They're key arteries for Hide and Go Seek Tag. From the deck you just have to shimmy up the drainpipe and use the molding over the French doors as a foothold while you push through the loose screen in the window. Sometimes I climb in that way even when there's no reason to. I just like the feeling of it. It's sort of exciting. Romantic maybe. It reminds me of *The Adventures of Tom Sawyer*, which my dad used to read me when I was little and I couldn't get to sleep. I could never sleep right. Even when I was a baby.

So I was balanced on this narrow piece of molding, clinging to my windowsill with purple fingers, when I felt a thump on my leg. I looked down at the pavement behind our deck, but there was nobody there. Turning back to the window, I spied a little something below me on the deck. A little something orange. A carrot.

"Who's there?" I called out, figuring it must be Donald Diamond or one of the other neighborhood twerps. No answer. "Fuck you very much for the carrot," I yelled. No answer. I looked over my shoulder again. This time I nearly fell and broke my neck. Still no one there. But I could hear something. A wet coughing sound, like someone crinkling newspaper. The way my grandmother used to sound before she passed away. I climbed down to the deck and picked up the fallen carrot. It was only the middle part of what looked like a good-sized carrot. Only it had been neatly carved into the shape of a hare. I eyed it half a minute in wonder, running my thumb along the back of its ears and down its spine. I heard the coughing again, only now it sounded closer and maybe tinged with laughter. Coming from directly below me. I squatted down and peeked through the floorboards. There was the freckled dome of an old man squatting by my garage door.

I cupped my hands to the wood beneath my feet. "Who are you?" I asked. The man looked up startled, realizing he was spotted.

"Why are you breaking into your own house?" he coughed.

"I asked you first," I said back.

"Okay," he answered, going into another fit of the coughs.

"There's a hose down there," I told him. "Turn it on and drink from it."

He slowly bent over and twisted the knob. The hose made a hissing sound and began to spit. He picked up the end and held it carefully, leaning forward to sip. Still he managed to soak the front of his shirt, which was made of a thin pale-blue material that went see-through in an instant. His crotch got some too and it looked like he pissed himself. He looked up to say thank you. I think we made eye contact through a crack in the boards. I asked his name again. He told me to call him Mister Reese.

"Why did you throw this carrot at me?" I tossed it over the railing.

"That's two questions," he shook his head. "Not fair. Why are you breaking into your own house? Did you lose a key?"

"That's two questions, too," I said. Then, "I was avoiding someone."

"Ahhhh," he went, like he understood the situation completely. "I'll leave you to continue avoiding her then . . ."

He walked out from under the deck and started off again, in the opposite direction of where his house is located. I walked over to the railing to watch him. Without looking over his shoulder, he called out to me. "Carrots make people see better," he said. "And we can all find ourselves pretty blind from time to time."

I watched him round a bend and head up one of the little stairwells. As he began to disappear, I noticed he was wearing slippers. Then the French doors snapped open behind me. I flinched and turned around. My mother. Her hair was wet and sparkly. She was dressed up for work. Her work clothes always make her shoulders look too big for her little head. It's funny. She hugged me without saying anything. I had no choice but to hug her back, even though I felt sort of awkward about it. I hugged her gently, patting her shoulder blade with my hand. She felt skinny. When we were finished hugging, she stepped back and looked me up and down. "Who were you talking to?" she said.

"Nobody," I told her. "Myself."

She went off to work and I went down to check out the little orange rabbit. He was broken in pieces on the asphalt. The only part I could still recognize was his face. It looked sad.

~

Yesterday was Saturday and I went to the hospital. I fell off my bike. I was riding on Springlake Way and my front wheel came off. I flew over the handlebars. I bit my lip when I hit the ground. Or maybe on the way down. Anyway, my teeth went right through and came out the other side. There was blood everywhere, bright red like food coloring. But it didn't hurt that bad. I didn't cry or anything. A woman and her little boy were driving past and they stopped to help me. I told them my house was only a block away and I could make it on my own, but they insisted. When I got home my dad was busy on the computer, burning CD's for his jukebox. I went into his office still bleeding all over my T-shirt. Dad freaked out. He made me go into the kitchen. He thought I was going to ruin the carpet.

Dad drove me to GBMC, where they stitched me up. The thread they used is black and prickly and it sticks out of my bottom lip like overgrown facial hairs. My dad snapped at me twice on the ride home because I couldn't stop touching my stitches. I still keep fidgeting with them even as I'm writing this. When I told my dad I couldn't stop, he shook his head in disgust. He told me to sit on my hands if I couldn't control myself. Then we stopped off at Princeton Sports and got a new bolt-thingy for the wheel of my bike.

Today he asked me if I wanted to go riding with him. My dad used to ride bikes a lot, before he got older and fat. He looked kind of sad when he asked me and I didn't react right away, like it was important to him or something. I didn't really want to get up from the couch where I was watching cartoons, but we don't get a lot of quality hang-out time together, so I guess I felt sort of compelled to go. I told him about a waterfall I know on the Jones Falls near Hampden. Me and the Beaster Bunny sometimes go there to smoke blunts, but I didn't tell Dad about that. I just said it was pretty and all.

Dad put on his helmet and we rode out. I never wear my helmet because the way a bike helmet sits on top of your head reminds me of a penis. The mushroom cap part, where you get circumcised. It's dorky looking is all. My father strapped on his old bike helmet from the seventies though. It used to be red but now it's faded purple. It makes him look like a dildo . . .

He got real tired on the way down to the falls. He had to stop and catch his breath. I got impatient waiting for him and asked if he wanted to go back. He acted sort of pissy and agitated about my suggestion. A little further down Roland Avenue he saw me popping wheelies and told me to stop showing off.

We got to Round Falls and he insisted on locking up our bikes, even though I doubt very much if anybody would steal them while we were standing so close by. But my dad doesn't trust people, I guess. So we locked up our bikes.

Round Falls is a pretty sweet place to hang out. It's right in the city, but not many people know about it. There is a little wood deck with a bench you can sit on, which was apparently donated by some guy my father used to do business with. There was a plaque with the guy's name on it and my father told me he knew him . . . I like it there anyway . . . It's a good spot. Right beneath the horseshoe of falling water is a deep pool that flattens back out into the stream and keeps bubbling on down to the harbor. People swim at Round Falls supposedly, even though the river is dirty. There are always a lot of cigarette butts and forties lying around. Sometimes needles. If you look up the hill every fifteen minutes or so you can see the light rail roll past. I like that . . . Today I saw a mallard. His feathers looked dirty. If my mother was with us, she probably would have named him. And maybe made up a story about him. I decided to call him Sam but my father thinks that stuff is for babies so I named him to myself, secretly.

Anyway, I guess Dad thought Round Falls was pretty cool at first. He spent most of his time trying to figure out the history of the waterfall, which is man-made and used to have something to do with all the abandoned mills in the neighborhood. I couldn't give a shit about who made it, but I pretended to be interested for his sake.

After a while I started reading the graffiti, some of it out loud when I thought it was funny. My dad HATES graffiti. He becomes fixated when he sees it on a wall. That's what happened today. He couldn't get over all the graffiti. On the deck and on the wall by the river and even on some of the trees. It put him in a real sour mood. I told him not to let it spoil his good time, but he couldn't stop thinking about it. They found graffiti inside the Great Pyramid, I told him. And it was a standard form of communication in ancient Rome.

He was already angry though. I shouldn't have defended vandalism, that annoyed him, even if I was just trying to say he shouldn't let it bother him. My father decided to give me a lecture. On private versus public property and civil contracts and such. He acted like *I* was the one who had written it. Like I was responsible for the very existence of all graffiti within city limits . . . Truth is, I could have written some of it. Beats me. I write on just about everything when I'm bored. Benches, curbs, desks, my shoes, my own skin. But it's not like he had any reason to persecute me for it on our bike ride.

He lectured me anyway. The slightest sound out of my mouth he took for an argument. I was afraid to even hiccup or cough. He was secretly pissed about something else, I figured . . . My dad gets angry about everything. Even to the point of being angry with me when he thinks I'm being angry. All the while I'm not usually angry, but frustrated, nervous, excited, or scared . . . And when my father gets mad—he's always slightly pissed off about something—his eyebrows go all nutso. My father has tremendous eyebrows. Like caterpillars mating. They seem to grow larger and closer with age. And when he's upset they flex up high on his forehead. Like antennae. Or horns. He looks down at you and his brows cover his eyes like a visor. They take on a life of their own. Feelers. They probe deep into my soul and try to strangle it. The whole thing makes me highly uncomfortable. And that's what happened today. So we rode home pretty much in silence. On the way, I tried to dream up a fantasy story about Sam the duck. I couldn't.

~

When I was little I used to get off on cutting up living things that were much smaller than me . . . I particularly relished mowing the lawn . . .

If you listen closely while cutting the grass, you can hear each blade's tiny scream. "STOP IT!" they shout. "LET US GROW!"

~

When I was a kid I used to tell my mother that I remembered living in her womb. I'd make up whole stories about my time in there. Living inside her, eating her protein, floating around in her fluids, kicking her, scratching like cave paintings into the walls of her uterus. She thought it was cute. I was lying, of course. There were other stories I'd often pretend to remember, true stories, or at least partly true stories, although I didn't actually remember them. Stuff, family history I'd put together from the anecdotes spun by my folks and their friends at get-togethers. Like my baptism at the Basilica, when my godfather supposedly decided to come out of the closet and leave his wife and children, who were all much older than me. I don't have any memory if that was the way it happened, how could I, being less than a month old? But sometimes it seems like I do remember. Because I've heard about it so much.

Likewise, I'm not sure if I remember the time I got stung in the eyeball by a yellowjacket after trying to pet it on its fuzzy, striped behind. My tear duct swelled up like a ping-pong ball, I think I cried a lot and for a few tense minutes I was locked out of the house, but do I really remember that stuff? Same goes for the spinal tap I received as an infant to combat a mysteriously high fever I'd developed. I can sort of picture the giant needle, but I know the memory is not real. My first REAL memory, the only one I can be sure of, isn't any of those.

The moment I first became aware of myself and the world I'd be stuck in for the rest of my life involved a spray hose, two dogs, a babysitter whose name I've long since forgotten, and her friend. I remember having a vicious case of diarrhea. Hot liquid shits . . . My stomach must've always been pretty fucked up if my first memory involves poop . . . Anyway, my babysitter must have carried me outside because that's where I remember coming to. There were dogs licking me, nipping at the feces running down my leg. It was our retriever, who died soon afterward, and the neighbors' dachshund, who must have been drawn by the smell. They terrified me, lapping at my skin. I was shrieking and crying and squirting furiously. A little brown fountain. My babysitter—who was this person?—was busy hosing me down with a fierce nozzle, washing the shit from my legs and trying to scare off the dogs at the same time. It didn't work. More shit kept gushing. More and more. From where? I didn't understand. I have distrusted my body ever since.

Everyone was frantic. The hounds kept licking up and down my tiny legs, jockeying for position. They had gone absolutely rabid for my turds. I could see it in their eyes, their teeth. Their doggy tongues were enormous. I couldn't stop screaming over the sound of that hose and those monster animal tongues. My babysitter's friend was laughing her head off, cackling, rolling around on the grass some distance away. My babysitter was laughing too, but trying to keep it in control.

Laughing out of despair, I guess. I couldn't stop crying. And the dogs wouldn't go away. And the waste poured out with no end . . . Then my head folded back up on me and I don't remember anything really, nothing I can think of, until my first swimming lesson or my first day at school. I remember I didn't want to be there.

~

Dinner at my mother's house is always unpredictable. Like last week for instance we were having pork chops and sauerkraut and mashed potatoes and red wine. The A/C was on the fritz and everyone was sweating. I turned on the fan and opened the windows, but that didn't do the trick. It was still hot as hell. And you could hear the cicadas buzzing away outside. It was loud as fuck. My sisters got tipsy on one glass of wine and Katie kept trying to make Thomas Angel eat sauerkraut. He didn't like it. He hissed and went under the table. My mother was chasing her wine with light beer. She kept refilling her glass. She couldn't stop whining about my father, what a bastard he is, and Kelly kept defending him. I tried not to listen and watched a shitty pop culture trivia show instead, but the phenobarbital I'd taken earlier was giving me a headache and I was having trouble understanding the questions. Robby, the Beaster Bunny, had gotten me the pills from his work where they prescribe them to dogs that have seizures. Robby came by during dinner and ate half a pork chop. He had just gotten an eyebrow ring. Katie liked it and asked my mother if she could have one too. My mother said she didn't care what any of us did to our bodies anymore, but I could tell she didn't think much of the idea. The Beaster Bunny pretended to go upstairs for a piss and left a bag of herb on my desk before leaving. He owed it to me from last week. The second he was gone I charged upstairs to make sure he had left it. When I came downstairs from taking bong hits, my mother was looking pretty spent, leaning on her elbow like it was a crutch. Her friend Susie came by with sherbet and blueberries for dessert. Upon seeing my mother's condition, she took out a bottle of something and gave her one. My mother swallowed the pill with red wine. Her lips were looking purple. I suggested she go take a nap. She accused me of being just like my father. I tried not to respond. It took about five minutes for the heat to turn the carton of sherbet into a pink saccharine sludge. I ate some anyway. Katie gave her bowl to Thomas Angel the cat, who jumped up on the counter to eat it. He lapped that shit up like liquid crack. It made him hyper. He started chasing around after a fattened moth that had flown in the window, drawn by the light of the television. He killed the moth and ate it. One of the wings was stuck to his mouth. I tried to take it off and he freaked out. He ended up knocking over my mom's big glass bowl of kraut, which broke in pieces against the tile. Susie tried cleaning it up, but my mother wouldn't let her and stooped over to do it herself. Kneeling on the floor, Mom began to cry because the bowl used to belong to her dead mother. Susie and the twins tried to console her, but she wouldn't stop cleaning the mess. She cut her thumb on a shard of glass and the blood started to flow pretty heavily, mixing in with all that shredded cabbage and sliced apple and vinegar. I took off my T-shirt and gave it to her as a bandage. Kelly made fun of me for being so scrawny. I gave her the finger. My mom gave me a teary-eyed stare and, sucking on her wound, she asked me how I had grown up to be so "vulgar." I got angry and told her to sober up and asked why she always had to act like such a whiny bitch. "Don't you call me a BITCH!" she shrieked. "I am your MOTHER!" I tried to explain that I hadn't called her a bitch, just asked her why she kept *acting* like one. Susie gave me the evil eye when I said that. Story of my life. I'm so misunderstood. By this time Katie had called my father and told him my mother was bleeding. He told Katie to give me the phone. He blamed me for not watching after my mother properly, then he asked me if I'd been giving my little sister drugs on account of the way Katie was apparently slurring her words on the phone. I hung up on him. He didn't call back. My mother yelled at me for hanging up on my father. I don't have any respect, she said, and I'm out of control, and what kind of example am I setting for my sisters? They're both already grade-A sluts, I countered, citing as evidence a blow job rumor I heard last week involving Kelly and Jon Shaver. My mom's dykey friend was massaging her shoulders at this point. She told me to watch my mouth. I was in a room full of ladies, she said. I called her a cunt and stomped upstairs. I called Robby's cell phone, looking for a ride out of there, anywhere; I was willing to pay for gas. But Robby didn't pick up his phone. When I came back down Katie and Kelly were fighting about Jon Shaver, who they were both apparently crushing on. Katie glared at me and stuck her tongue out like a goddamn five-year-old. Like I was responsible for the sucking of Jon Shaver's dick! Exasperated, I grabbed one of my mother's beers and rode out on my skateboard. There were fireflies everywhere, blinking. The cicadas were droning away all around me, shrill and constant. I went to the molehill and sat down, but the moles were all hiding, deep inside their mound. I puked a little against the inside of my teeth. I spit it out on the dirt. I rolled a sloppy joint and smoked it as best as possible, but it kept going out and pieces of pot kept falling out the ends. Finally things began to chill out, but hordes of mosquitoes were sucking the hell out of me. So I went back home. When I got inside, Susie had gone home. Thank god. My mother and my sisters were sitting around in their pajamas, all curled up in front of the TV. Kelly was sucking her thumb. Katie was chewing her nails.

My mother's hand was all wrapped up in gauze. There was a dark red dot on the bandage, where the blood had begun to coagulate. They asked me to sit down with them and watch *Desperate Housewives.* I hate that show but I sat down anyway. Apparently they had ordered a pizza. They asked if I would mind answering the door when it came. Big black moths kept crawling on the TV screen, but no one seemed to notice. I thought it was going to turn my stomach again, but it didn't. The door rang and I paid for the pizza, happy to hijack part of the tip. And that was basically a regular night around here . . .

~

One of the Alateen rooms I used to go to was in the basement of a Methodist church and during the day it doubled as a day-care center. There were a billion toys tucked away in the corner and the rug was made of Astroturf in primary colors with a hopscotch lane running down the middle. There was kiddie art all over the walls. The first time I went there I spotted a page from a child's coloring book tacked up on the corkboard. My eyes were just drawn to it for some reason. I stared at the thing constantly from then on, whenever I was bored. I was always bored. The picture was up there all year long. I never stopped staring . . . The page was colored in very neatly, I thought, especially for a child. (When I was little I could never stay in the lines. My crayon just went all over the page, in thick messy streaks. I sucked at coloring books . . .) In the middle of the picture there was an island, lurching up brown and green from a pale blue sea scattered with whitecaps. On the island was a red brick home settled on the edge of what looked like a fort with a lighthouse. There was a patch of puffy treetops that the kid had drawn little polka-dot apples inside. I thought the apples were a nice touch. Seabirds surged over the ocean, where there was a sailboat and a small tug enjoying the weather. Big blue clouds like whales floated over the scene, looking down. In the forefront, on the shore, were lumps of brown sand covered in dune grass.

Like I said, everything was filled in very neatly, except for the blank white sky, which made the drawing seem incomplete and sort of frightened me. At the very top, printed across that sky, the page had been titled in red crayon, all in caps: "MOM PLACE!"

[*The next three and a half pages of Miles's journal are missing and unable to be transposed for your reading pleasure. Sorry for the inconvenience. The following entry is only a fragment at the end of a larger entry. —Ed.*]

. . . and if there are things like that in the world, feelings . . . no matter how short-lived . . . but feelings like that buzzing away inside the folds and tissues of a person's brain, about another person no less, or about anything for that matter, about life and living and being alive in general I guess, well then I thought the world was okay maybe and I would open up my bag of pretzels and enjoy them in the pool.

~

My head is KILLING me.

The Beaster Bunny called yesterday to inform me of some ketamine he beasted from the animal hospital. Ketamine is a feline tranquilizer, but it gets people fucked up too and makes them hallucinate. Or so I had heard. Beaster Bunny was hanging out with his Jewish friend Dradel from the art school and also a couple chicks they were trying to fuck. There were only two girls though, which kind of left me out of the loop.

But they wanted to snort K and drink beer and they needed somewhere to go. Honestly, I was exhausted from skating all day. I'd already planned on taking some bong hits and riding my bike up to Blockbuster maybe, then calling it a night. But, as usual, I suck at saying "No." So we ended up breaking into my old house, which is easy as fuck. Like Simple Simon . . .

The house was empty of course so there was nothing to do but get drunk and listen to this cornball classic rock station on the contractors' staticky boom box. I didn't mind though, some of the tunes weren't so bad and one of the bitches, Dradel's girl Sonja, was actually pretty hot. We had basically the same haircut, Sonja and me, but hers was dyed black on one side. And she had earrings in her face like Robby. Still, she had a nice body and I dug the way she did her makeup. But I didn't stand a chance. She was all over Dradel, who was like twice my size and drove a Land Rover, even though I suspect he was borrowing it from his mother because I found a Jewish Mothers Association pamphlet in the back seat with an events schedule from some synagogue in Mount Washington. Besides, my lip was still all busted and stitched up in gnarly black thread. So I didn't even try.

Robby got me to jury-rig a table from a piece of plywood and a pair of horses that were lying up against the wall. We stood around it to play Flip Cup. Since I was the odd man out I had to switch sides every game. That means whichever side I was on inevitably lost because they had an extra player. So we gave it up after a while and decided to just drink on our own. Fine with me, I was getting myself hammered. Eventually we started bumping the ketamine. I got a little less than everyone else, because Robby had promised to get the girls "really spun." He swore he'd steal more though and I could have it. Whatever's clever, I told him, and did whatever he gave me.

I didn't feel anything special at first, just more and more drunk. Sonja and her friend were already pretty fucked up though, giggling and giving each other the crazy eyes. They weirded me out. Robby was trying to ease the tension I guess, so he rolled up a blunt and we went out back to smoke it.

There's a tree alongside the house covered in these big brainy fruits called Osage oranges. They're fluorescent green and stinky and full of this gummy ooze that starts to pus out from the rotten parts when they've been on the ground for too long. The squirrels LOVE these things. They grind them up in little bits and carry the seeds off to their nests. I used to throw them at cars on the street. Otherwise they're completely worthless, I think. The girls found a few uses for them though . . .

They kept picking the wretched things up. They were amazed that such a fruit even existed. "They're beautiful," they kept saying. "They look . . . prehistoric." And "Touch it! Ewww! Touch it! It's a BRAIN! Look! A BRAIN!" Osage oranges do look a lot like brains, but I'm not sure what's so beautiful or prehistoric about brains. Robby and Dradel were trying to distract the girls, get them to go back inside. No dice on that score. These chicks were obsessed. I just leaned back on the old lacrosse net, watching. I was starting to get a pretty good head going. I couldn't stop laughing for one thing.

The bugs up in the trees were buzzing so loud it sounded like someone screaming. I watched Sonja and her friend split open an Osage orange with their fingers. They started smearing the pus on each other's bodies. Like paint. I swear. I've never seen semi-hot chicks engaged in such fruit-loopy behavior. Robby was looking pretty fucked up himself at this point. He'd given up on the prospect of fucking I guess and sat down on the lawn. Dradel kept trying to take Sonja's hand though. I don't think he was that fucked up yet. He still had his heart set on screwing. Sonja just kept smearing the green gook on his face and cackling. Dradel was getting pretty annoyed. I just kept drinking. I couldn't tell if the beers had gotten warm or if it was just my mouth. I didn't care much either way. I couldn't stop drinking. My head started to spin. I felt a sudden urge to look in the mirror. I had to see myself. I tried to walk in the house, but I couldn't do it. It felt like my body was missing, like I was just a head walking around on a pair of feet. Like one of those little mushroom guys from Super Mario Bros. I decided to just lie there against the lax goal, watching fireflies and getting bitten by bugs.

When the girls started eating pieces of the fruit, Dradel grabbed Robby and decided they were all going home. I don't blame him. You're not supposed to eat that shit. They were feeding it to each other. They wanted to bring some inside the house. And cook it. Fuck that, I said. Or thought. I'm not sure which. Those bitches were crazy . . .

Robby and Dradel tried to get me up but I mumbled something about how I was gonna stay there and sleep in my old bedroom. After I heard their car pull out of the driveway, I threw up. A lot. I had been holding it in. For the sake of the girls, I guess. Whatever. This morning I woke up on the lawn, covered in bug bites and vomit. My head was still spinning. The sun was high already and my vision was full of purple spots. I sat up and rubbed my fists into my eye sockets real hard. Blinking, I noticed two gray bunny rabbits on the lawn, so close I could touch them. They were picking at my vomit and the little green leftovers of the Osage oranges for food. I farted. And they panicked. I had interrupted them. I was sorry when they ran away. I had scared them. It was all my fault.

~

I was rolling down the sidewalk on my skateboard, carefully counting each cicada carcass as they crunched beneath my wheels, when Mister Reese's hatchback pulled up right in front of me. I jumped in my skin. I was afraid he would notice, I didn't want him to know I was scared. I took my foot off the board and stood there, trying to look tough. The old man got out of the car holding a brown paper bag. The bag was wiggling, wriggling, beating like a heart. He tipped his hat to me. I waved back timidly, with a flick of the wrist. I couldn't take my eyes off that bag. He must have noticed because he chuckled. His smile looked . . . wicked? A grimy chill ran up my spine. One of his teeth was dead black.

He reached into the bag and yanked out a snow white rat by its tail, which was fleshy and pink like a worm. I probably jumped again, I'm not sure. The poor animal thrashed around a bit before Mister Reese shoved it back in the bag. He tipped his hat once more and headed inside, quietly chuckling to himself. I stood there a while, alone on the sidewalk, feeling stupid and weird about life in the world that I live in.

~

I went to see my physician today. My pediatrician actually. I still go to a pediatrician. I had asked my mother to make the appointment. She looked worried when I asked her. It's no secret that I hate going to the doctor. I don't usually volunteer for a checkup. I told her my allergies were acting up. I was lying. I pretended to sneeze. I'm not sure if she bought it, but she made the phone call anyway. This morning she left money on the counter for cab fare and the co-pay. I called Russian Stan for a ride.

What had really been bothering me was a painful rash that had been getting worse every day for the last week. I used to get hives when I was a kid, in big puffy chains across my torso and wrists. But this was different. The hives would go away after a few hours. The doctors said they were caused by stress. This new rash was different though, achy and budding. And it stuck around. It was a darker pink too, almost brown in places. It was living in my left armpit and the fleshy canal between my thighs and my testicles. The skin down there was all chapped. There were cracks like coin slots developing on the surface. I wondered if it was shingles. Or if my first brush with oral sex had given me some kind of freaky VD. I wondered if I could get any painkillers. The world felt heavy.

Stan dropped me off at Saint Joseph's in Towson. The building was cold inside. I pretended to read *Highlights* magazine in the waiting room. I tried to look for the hidden pictures, but it gave me a headache, so I gave up. Instead I sat behind the magazine and used it as a prop so I wouldn't have to make eye contact with anyone. But I couldn't help looking at them anyway.

There was a little boy waiting with his mother. The boy's face looked green. He kept moaning. He wanted a lollipop. His mother tried to shush him. She buried his head in her lap. He bit her. She had to scold him. I pretended not to notice. I was embarrassed for her. I hate kids. But then again, adults suck too. Probably worse. I felt so depressed that I nearly got up and left. I thought about running off to the woods and letting the rash take over, gradually turning me into a monster. That's when they called my name. The nurse led me into a little room. She put me on a scale. Apparently I'd lost weight. She was concerned. She looked to me for a response. I apologized. "I'm sorry," I said. I didn't know what else to say. Then the doctor came in.

After checking my heartbeat, Doctor Blum asked about my parents. I told him they were "great." He wasn't listening though. I could have told him they were cannibals and he wouldn't have raised an eyebrow . . .

I wasn't sure how to bring up the subject of my rash. I was embarrassed about it. I figured he'd see it and ask me about it when he went to check out my balls anyway. I hate when they do that. It always makes me tense up and laugh. I can't help it. It's an awkward situation and I'm ticklish. I'm afraid I'll catch a wood or something. He didn't do it this time. Instead he lifted up my chin and looked in my eyes. He asked me, "What is wrong with you now? I saw you less than six months ago . . ."

"Nothing really," I started. "I mean I doubt it's serious . . ."

"You let me be the judge of that, Miles. Now, spit it out already." He's such a know-it-all. I was kind of surprised when he didn't call me "Retard," not that he ever has before. It just seemed to fit at the time . . .

I lifted my arm and showed him the rash. He asked me how bad was the pain, on a scale of one to ten. I guessed a seven at first. Then I changed my answer to six. That seemed more appropriate somehow. Doctor Blum held my arm like a puppet's and stared deep into my armpit, which is just starting to get hairy. He made a few little chirps of agreement, *mmhhmmm, mmhhmmm*, like he was reading an editorial or something.

"And there's more," I said, pointing to my waist. "Down there." He dropped my arm and stretched out the elastic waistline on my boxers so he could get a good look at my crotch. He only peeked for half a second before he let the elastic snap back against my belly.

"Fungus," he said with authority.

"Fungus? What do you mean 'fungus'?"

"I mean you have a fungal infection."

"How would I get . . . that?" I was confused.

"Oh, fungus is everywhere." He hiked his thumb over his shoulder. "Out there, in here, on me, on you, everywhere."

"Definitely on me?" I asked.

"Definitely on you."

"Um, okay . . . Why?"

"It crops up in places on your body that don't get enough sunlight. Don't worry, you don't have to change your deodorant or anything." I could tell I was supposed to be relieved. A fungal infection is good news, I gathered. Better than VD. Or shingles. Or plague.

"Would a fungal infection ache like this?" I still wanted painkillers.

"It could. Your lymph nodes are pretty swollen. And the skin is broken in places from chafing." He spoke to me like I was a child. I could tell I wasn't getting any Percocet. He prescribed me an over-the-counter cream.

I called Stan from the pay phone outside. "Diagnosis on rash was okay?" he asked.

"Swell," I told him. And we took off for Rite Aid where Stan waited in the car while I ran inside for some Micatin. Then I had him get me a six-pack up the street and slipped him an extra ten.

When I got home I squirted the chilly cream on my palms and began to massage it into the sensitive red flesh around my crotch and my armpit. It hurt pretty badly, but I was still embarrassed for calling jock itch a seven on the pain scale.

The fungicide itself didn't burn the rash, but felt damp and mild. Naked, I hopped in bed with my six-pack and picked up the remote control. I muted the television and started to watch a show about the tiny fish that swim alongside of great white sharks, nibbling parasites off their skin. Pilot fish, they're called. The mattress felt moist beneath me. My skin smelled gross. I was kind of relieved though. For once in my life, I knew exactly what was wrong with me. I had a fungus growing on my body. We all did. But mine had just gotten out of control and now I was going to fix it. I was mildly blissful, to tell you the truth. The fan whispered and tickled my rash. There was nothing left to do for the day, so I lay in bed completely still except for the breath washing in and out of my lungs. I felt mossy and organic. Beneath the whir of the fan blades, I almost thought I could hear myself growing. Like a forest.

~

I'm not sure that my mother is capable of relaxation. She has absolutely no grasp on the concept of serenity. She just can't unwind. But she likes to make a big deal of talking about relaxing, that's for sure. I think that's the only way she can do it. It's kind of sad, if you think about it. Like on Fridays, she'll come home and have a cigarette, maybe a couple light beers—which make her slightly edgy—and then she'll drink four cups of coffee. She puts ice in it. She says it helps her "relax." She even drinks a cup right before bed. And while she's supposedly trying to chill out, she'll scurry around the house scrubbing the counters, the walls, trying to force-feed us, trying to make us drink milk.

She's constantly making lists out loud on her fingers. *First I'll make coffee, then I'll call work, then go to the store, then cook, then serve, then chew, swallow, digest, wish on a star, and go to sleep before I have to wake up again and make coffee . . .* Always listing off the groceries we have in the fridge out loud, over and over, in case we'd forgotten how to look for ourselves. Then she'll go around turning the lights on and off. Opening windows. Toying with the A/C. Adjusting the blinds. Nothing's ever perfect enough. If she catches you watching television, she'll come in and try to put a pillow behind you, or prop your feet up. She'll cover you with a blanket, even during summer when the humidity hangs around like a bad odor.

First thing she says when she comes home at the end of the week is always something like, "Now I'm going to relax. All weekend. All I have to do is relax. Don't you think it's beautiful outside? Maybe I'll go and look. Does anybody want a sandwich? I have to make a phone call. Whoa, this floor is dirty."

As soon as the stars come out, she takes the chance to rush outside and make a wish. Meanwhile the only thing visible up there is satellites and airplanes. Because of the light from the city. I regularly remind her of this, but she likes to wish on them anyway.

"All I'm going to do is *relax*." She says it at least forty times a weekend probably. No joke. "I just *love* the weekend. All I have to do is *relax*."

"Why don't you do it, then?" I'll snort. I'm such an asshole.

But seriously, I imagine that if you're really relaxing you don't have to talk about it. You don't even THINK about it . . . It's like she can't think of anything else to say. And she has to say something, but the only thing on her mind is how "relaxed" she's planning to get, how great it will be if it ever happens. I doubt very much that she's ever been completely relaxed. Not even during sleep. Asleep, she's all hog-grunt snoring and hacking chest coughs. She doesn't know the meaning of REM sleep . . . My mom sleeps with the TV on very loud. She's like me, she can't fall asleep if it's quiet, so she watches TV in bed. It's the only time she can sit still during a show. If you come in and hit the power button while she's snoring, she'll wake up. The rest of the day she can't even sit through normal shows. She's all twenty-four-hour news channels in the background and fidgeting. She can't sit through a movie. She never ever, ever listens to music. It makes her nervous. She's always waiting for the chorus . . . Sometimes she'll go to bed three or four times in a night, never sleeping, purely at a loss for things to do.

Maybe I'll sleep, she thinks. No, not yet. Maybe a cigarette? Wish on another satellite? Maybe I'll run the vacuum? Maybe I won't run the vacuum and instead dream up some other task?

I think she drinks in bed at night, naked and sweating in front of her fan. I find empties in her closet. She's a whole bundle of nerves. Can't clear her head. Her brain never stops moving. It's like a bumblebee. Or a shark. I wish to god she'd smoke weed.

It's too bad she doesn't, too. If anyone deserves to chill out, it is my mother. She works hard as HELL all week long. Even at night somebody is always calling from work. They can't show up tomorrow. Their dog is sick. They're hungover. The bus missed their stop. The terror alert is rising. The sky is falling . . . Ungrateful bastards. And us kids don't give her much time for proper relief either, that's for sure. Especially me, always getting in trouble. Always with the phone calls from school. Parent-teacher conferences. My probation officer. Another fistfight. More stitches. It's always something with me. I feel bad.

"I'm *so* relaxed," she says, ironing. "This is *such* a nice weekend. I'm just going to enjoy myself. I'm just going to relax. All weekend. Just relax."

I get annoyed with her. "I get it, Mom. You're going to relax. You already told me. It *is* a nice weekend to relax. When are you gonna get started already?"

I'm a nasty little shit. A bad person in most ways probably. You know, I try to do things for her. But she doesn't like to be waited on. Whenever we go out to eat, I swear she'd offer to clean off our table if only the restaurant would let her. I wish I could do something to help her chill out. The other day I slipped a phenobarbital into her coffee. I don't even think she noticed. She just went on scrubbing. And making phone calls. Lighting cigarettes. Coughing. "I'm just going to relax," she said. "All weekend. I'm so happy to be home. Maybe I'll go for a walk. After the dishes are done. Did you know we have apples in the fridge? And ice cream in the freezer? Pretzels in the cupboard? Do you want me to order a pizza? How about I make you a tuna sandwich? I'm just going to take it easy, I think . . ."

Then she'll pour a few more cups of coffee. And run through another list. And try to relax . . .

~

Those goddess lips! Eyelids like flower petals! Lashes like wet leaves! Hair like golden honey dripping off her beautiful empty head! Awww, fuck it. I refuse to let poetry slip from this tongue . . . Poetry is for suckers . . . It always feels like a confession. But then again, this is supposed to be a journal . . . and therefore secret . . .

In case you haven't figured it out already, I saw Ashley Vidal today. I went up to the pool. On the table at the gate where the sign-in sheet is, sat her little brother Kevin. He was wearing two black dress socks on his forearms. Puppets with white buttons for eyes and purple yarn for lips. Kevin had glued plastic miniature collectible baseball helmets to the place where the toes usually go to simulate sideways ball caps. He was putting on a show for whoever would watch. I was the only one standing there. I think Kevin is funny. The socks were dissing each other in Ebonics, talking mad shit. Ashley came out the gate in a bathing suit and an oversized T-shirt, dripping, trying to suction water from her ear.

"Mom just phoned," she warned Kevin. "You have a doctor's appointment. She says I have to walk you straight home. To make you sure you don't run off."

Kevin groaned.

"Fuckin-a," she told him. "Let's go. *Now.* I'm trying to tan."

"I'm not going unless Retard walks back with us," he whined. Kevin likes me.

Ashley looked at me sheepishly and apologized. Then she turned back to Kevin. "Let's go," she told him. "Now."

"I don't mind going for a walk," I said. I gave her a fake little smile to show what a swell, easygoing dude I was.

"You sure you don't mind?"

Was she kidding?

"Naw, I don't mind."

We walked her brother home. He kept picking up cicadas and she kept taking them from him. On the way back she pointed to one of the carcasses on the ground.

"Those things are so foul," she said.

"I think they're molting," I told her. I wasn't sure.

"What's . . . *molting*?"

"Like, shedding their skin."

"Gross," she said. "It looks like they're dying to me."

"I think they die after they mate," I said, trying to sound real smart. "Then the babies stay underground for seventeen years. And then they come up to mate. Or something."

"That's gross," she said. She started walking a little faster. I took the chance to check out the spot where her butt cheeks meet her long skinny legs. Damn was that little patch of skin mysterious. I could stare at that one spot for the rest of my life. I was starting to lag behind. I tried to catch up.

"So," I started, not sure what to say. "Um . . . You wanna get in the sauna?"

"I don't like it in there," she answered. "It makes me sweat."

I had to bite my tongue to keep from saying DUH . . . Ashley was so clueless and innocent.

"Yeah . . . But it feels real good when you jump in the pool afterward."

Next thing you know we were back at the gate to the pool. I had left my towel on the ground. I picked it up. I kind of flexed when I did it. I was hoping she'd notice my abs. She didn't.

Before heading over to her seat she told me thanks for helping with her little brother. "He can be *such* a pain," she told me. "I hate him."

I wanted to sit next to her, but I didn't. I sat a couple chairs down. She took off her T-shirt and put on her headphones. And a towel over her face. I watched her for a while from behind my sunglasses. I watched a bead of sweat drip off her belly, onto her chair, then into the grass and presumably the earth below.

Eventually, I got up and hit the diving board. I pulled just about every trick in my bag. Backflips, gainers, misty flips, rodeos, even the flying squirrel. I was hoping she'd notice. I'm not sure that she did. Finally, I gave up. I dipped out to smoke a joint on my father's back deck. I watched the crows for a while. They were sitting on a bulldozer in the empty lot, pecking dirt off the tires. I wondered how it tasted.

~

Ate crabs tonight at my cousin's and the Old Bay and the vinegar kept getting into the cuts where my cuticles should be—my fingertips look all haggard on account of biting my nails. Even as I write this it stings. But the stinging feels good. Like summertime. Like freedom and long afternoons. I'm at home now. The A/C is on high. I'm lying in my bed. I have a big smile on my face and I smell vaguely like a fish . . . Life is swell.

~

That banjo music keeps playing in my mother's neighborhood. Especially in the evenings, around sunset. Between that and the cicadas, it's like a genuine orchestra. Loud as shit. I like to smoke pot and listen. Sitting outside, with the moles.

~

I get really weirded out by my body. It disgusts me. I HATE IT. It's too scrawny, too short . . . I swear I'm finished growing. I'll always be some kind of fake dwarf. With dry, poofy hair. Nothing like the hair you see in movies. My hair, you can't even run a comb through. It's too thick. It hurts. So I don't even bother. And my legs are too twiggy. Skin and bones. Bird legs. My ankles stick out. Like I'm hiding walnuts in my socks. And my fingernails are always bloody. My chest is loaded with phlegm. When I cough, I sound like a bedridden geriatric. My teeth have already gotten yellow. My eyesight is terrible. But I never wear my glasses. I'm too proud. And by the way, I'm redundant as hell.

But more than anything, I hate my butthole. Really. I hate that the most. It's an evil little fucker. A ridiculous thing. Hiding out down there between my ass cheeks, beneath two layers of clothing. Letting farts slip out on the sly. Blowing them through its filthy lips . . . Come to think of it, I hate everyone's butthole. All of them. Buttholes in general. They're gross. And nobody gets them clean enough. The whole world is walking around with dirty anuses. Farting their brains out. And smiling all the while. Girls especially. From ear to ear. Telling each other how beautiful they look. Pretending nobody has to poop. Nobody just did. They live their whole lives that way. Until they realize they're starting to die . . . They're just waiting for the bad news . . . Then things start to get real . . . Farting is not so serious . . .

Well, maybe it's not just my body or assholes in general that I hate. Maybe I can't stand human bodies in general. They ooze into the world, they grow, they die, they rot, they stink . . . It's weird to even think of things like having a brain. An actual pulsing nerve center–type brain, like a brain-type brain inside your head. It's gross. And the other stuff too. Organs. Tendons, ligaments, muscles, bones . . . All pretty foul. If I could be part android, a bionic man like Robocop, with no asshole or guts or nagging brain, I'd do it in a second. Live forever, no nasty cancers, headaches, no more struggling to take a leak in the men's room at the ballpark, no more random boners. Robots have it made.

Shit, I'd rather be anything than a human. A dog or a squirrel. A thornbush even. At least you'd be too dumb to notice your body changing, dying, the foul condition it's in. Too dumb to realize you feel bad about things. But even then you'd get hungry. Or thirsty. Or sick . . . I guess I'd still rather be a cartoon than anything. Cartoons are the shiznit.

~

Sometimes I don't feel right and I have to go out and buy things to feel better. A videogame, a CD, DVD, comic book, new hat, sneakers, a skate deck, weed, a T-shirt, whatever. It's the only thing that will help. Like I feel empty inside, deflated. I need something to puff me back up again. Or I'll feel incomplete. I absolutely HATE this about myself. And about other people too.

I mean, seriously, what am I missing? What's wrong with me? Did cavemen have this problem? Not like the Flintstones who had money and gadgets of their own, but real cavemen. You know, naked uncivilized brutes. Maybe they did. Maybe they needed a shiny rock to feel secure. Or a cave painting. A skin. But what about the animals? They seem to do all right without money or toys . . . They eat, they shit, they fuck, play games, build nests . . . NESTS. Maybe that's it. Does a squirrel feel the same way about shoebox stuffing as I feel about shoes? Does a piece of string blow their hair back the way a new T-shirt does mine? I can't tell. But probably not. A nest is like shelter. And shelter is a PHYSICAL NEED, right? Not like a vintage comic. So why do us humans require all this other junk to feel good about life? We don't have a clue what to do with ourselves. It's a curse. On all of us. We're too smart for our own good, but never smart enough to be happy . . . All this fucking stimuli. Too easy to get bored. And boredom makes me feel uneasy about myself, about everything, just bad in general.

Sometimes I sit on the floor in the middle of my bedroom and surround myself with all the stuff I've collected. CD cases, comic books, skateboard wheels covered in flat spots . . . Like a pack rat alone in his hole. I'll just pick things up and look at them. The way I did with my stuffed animals when I was younger. But eventually I grow bored. I need to surround myself with new stuff all the time . . . Yuck . . . The very thought of it makes me feel desperate.

What if reincarnation really does exist? No, seriously. What if we, all of us, have actually been here before? Like possibly hundreds of times? Maybe that would explain why everyone is so bored.

~

Secret: Every time I happen to glance at a digital clock and see that it's just one number repeated (1:11, 2:22, 3:33, 4:44, 5:55, or 11:11)

I make a wish. Most people just do it at 11:11 but I really like making wishes so I take every chance I can get. Usually I wish that my mom will live a long, healthy life and be happy for most of it. But sometimes I wish for other things too. Like money or sex.

~

I'm sitting on my molehill in the afternoon, safely coated in insect repellent, with a bag of chronic on my lap, smoking a doobie. All is well. I guess. My mom's been depressed a lot lately. And really stressed out. And being a total bitch. Her bosses came to town from Texas or someplace to see how she's been managing the office. She thinks they're going to fire her for being too old. I try to comfort her, tell her not to worry about it. But what do I know anyway. I'm just a kid. Maybe she will get fired. Maybe she is too old . . . Besides that, the sun is up and there's a breeze. The firs on either side of me smell fragrant and the moles seem active. I think I can feel them moving around in the earth beneath my rear end. I'm not sure. I might be imagining things. But I've got a bag of the super dank and a full pack of cigarettes. And the stitches in my lip have begun to dissolve and fall out on their own. So life can't be all bad, I suppose.

I'm thinking about all these things and also about dreams. I'm wondering if coma patients have dreams. If they do, then being comatose might not be such a bad a way of life. It might even be more satisfying than real life. And maybe seem much longer in fact. It would certainly be more fantastic. And if the dreams are vivid, then WHY NOT enjoy a nice long coma? I'm not gonna lie to you, running all this kind of stuff through my head, I'm feeling a little zoned out . . .

But reality kicks in right off when I notice the fuzzy slippers at the foot of the mound. For all I know I could have been staring straight at them for an hour! A lifetime even! I jump in my skin, I panic. Fuzzy slippers! The whole situation is sketchy as hell. I try to stuff the herb in my pocket, but I'm sitting Indian-style and my shorts are drawn too tight across my thighs for me to get my hands inside. So I just stare at the ground for a while, hoping the slippers will walk away or dissipate if I stay perfectly still. After what feels like forever, I look up to see who it is.

He's just standing there, holding his hat in his hands, looking down at me . . . Mister Reese . . . "Hello there," he goes. He points to the bag in my lap. "You wouldn't mind letting me see that, would you, young man?"

My muscles tighten up. I'm preparing to take off at a sprint. Go shit in your hat, I want to tell him. "What are you gonna do, tell my mother?" I ask instead, getting all defensive. "She won't care. She's got her own problems, dude."

"As do we all," he sighs, and starts coughing. "As . . . do . . . we . . . all . . . " He looks left, then right, then over his shoulder, like to make sure nobody's watching. "No, siree. I won't be speaking to your mother. You've got my word on that score."

"Then what do you want to see it for, huh?"

"I'm an old-timer is all. And I imagine you kids get all the goodies. Curiosity is all . . . I can leave you alone if you like." He turns slowly and begins to shuffle off in his slippers.

I watch for a second, bewildered, and then something comes over me. I'm like, "Wait up. You can look. Here. Come back and check it out."

He slips a pair of reading glasses over his nose and squats down on the edge of the molehill. His joints creak like the Tin Man's. He must have arthritis I think. I watch as he carefully picks out a choice bud. He holds it over the baggie carefully, by the stem, so nothing falls off. He examines it for a moment, then brings it up to his snout and takes a deep breath. His nose hairs go all wild. It's gross.

I'm blushing. I can't help it. I'm not sure whether I'm smiling because A) I'm embarrassed someone will see me squatting on a molehill with this oddball geriatric, B) I'm way super proud of how heady my nuggets must look, or C) I just can't get over what a character this dude is. Maybe all three, I suppose. Or something else.

He looks up from the bag. His glasses slide down his nose and fall in the dirt. I lean forward and pick them up. He wipes them off on his shirt. "Those are some magnificent flower-tips you've acquired," he says. (FLOWER-TIPS!?! I think. How old is this guy!?!)

"Can you get any more?" he asks me.

And just like that I'm thinking this could be the start of a very profitable relationship.

"It depends on what you're looking for," I shrug, trying to come off like a pro. "As far as weight goes, you know?"

"Why don't you come over sometime and we can discuss it," he suggests. "I live right across the cul-de . . ."

"I know where you live," I say, cutting him off. A smile spreads across the old man's face. His teeth look big and fake. He nods once, tips his hat, and scuffles off.

~

Gary called me and asked if I would go to TGI Fridays with him and Kari and then to the Towson Commons for a movie. Amy was coming with Kari so it would be like a double date. I hadn't seen Amy since U.B. Fields and I was nervous. On top of that I had a pimple. I don't get zits very often. Puberty hasn't hit me hard enough yet I don't think. But when I do get one, I totally freak out. They're humiliating. I pick at them, squeeze them, try to push them back in my skin. I don't understand blemishes. They're so weird. Growths coming out of your face. It's freaky. What causes them? My mom says soda sometimes, but other times she says stress, and other times she says not washing up before supper or eating chocolate . . . So which is it?

Anyway I popped my pimple that morning, but by the middle of the day it looked even worse. Now it was a lumpy scab in the shape of a pimple. Bigger even. I didn't know what to do. I waited a few hours to see if it would go away. Of course, it did not. I picked off the scab, but that didn't help either. I was all ready to cancel and hide my head under a pillow for the rest of the week. Then I got an idea. I took out my pen knife and headed over to the mirror. I stuck the point into the scab and tugged the knife down the side of my face, giving myself a nice-sized vertical slash. It looked like something out of a pirate movie. A cut seemed less embarrassing than a pimple. I mean, I've heard that chicks dig scars, right? So now I was all ready to go. I was even admiring my new look in the mirror when the doorbell rang. I looked tough.

Kari's father picked us up in his Mercedes SUV and that made me feel nervous. I hate meeting parents. I'd hoped that Gary would've had Stan the Russian pick us up. I had money for it. My mom had slipped me three twenties when she heard I was going out to dinner with friends. With a girl even! She was ecstatic.

When I hopped in the back seat, Kari's dad tried to tell me a joke. "Two elephants are sitting in a bathtub," he said. "One turns to the other and asks for the soap. The other elephant says, 'No soap. Radio.'" I just smiled. I didn't get it. I don't think there was anything to get. I think that's the point. To make me feel stupid.

"Dad, you're *embarrassing* me," Kari groaned. "No one wants to hear your dumb joke . . . He tells it to everyone," she explained to the rest of us. "It doesn't make any sense. It's not supposed too. He tries to make strangers feel stupid."

After that awkward moment, everyone was pretty quiet for the rest of the ride, except for Kari's father who kept making jokes about the four of us eloping to Atlantic City, and Kari who kept whining for him to shut up. I sat next to Amy and could feel the shape of her hip against my bony thigh, but we didn't make eye contact even once. When I first sat down we both said "Hi." But we were staring at the back of the headrest when we said it.

At the restaurant, Kari looked way hot. Amy has a pretty face, but sort of plain, and she's a little pudgy. Not that I cared either way. I'm just saying is all, for the record. The girls were dressed almost identically: tight black pants, chunky heels, and halter tops, with their hair held up in ribbons. Like a uniform, I guess.

By the time we sat down, my grundle was already starting to sweat. I was nervous. I had a few phenobarbital in my pocket. I was already thinking about taking one. I would've offered them to the table, but I wasn't sure how it would go over. You can never tell with girls like that. Some of them are pro-booze, anti-drug. And some of them think you should wait until high school before you start eating pills. Or college even. It's weird.

Our waitress came dressed in a candy-striped shirt and snap-on suspenders that were all decked out in cheesy buttons. Strictly cornball stuff like, "SMILE A WHILE," and "MEAN PEOPLE SUCK," and "DON'T BOTHER ME I'M CRABBY." After she left, an awkward hush fell over the table. Kari unfolded her napkin and tried to break the ice. Looking right at me, she asked, "So, what happened to your face?"

I froze up. I hadn't thought that far ahead. "Oh, I, ah, cut myself," I said, trying to think up a lie. "Jumping over a fence." I thought that sounded pretty reasonable and I didn't know what else to say. I still hadn't even looked at Amy, but I thought I could feel her eyes on my cheek. They weren't reassuring.

Kari didn't miss a beat. "Why were you jumping over a fence?"

I mumbled something about the skate park being closed.

"You skateboard?" she asked. "Are you sponsored?"

"Yeah," I said, staring down at my chest. "By my mom."

Everyone laughed. Things felt a little more comfortable after that. I looked over at Amy and smiled. She smiled back. Our waitress returned with sodas and finger food: jalapeño poppers, mozzarella sticks, and chicken fingers. It all looked pretty much the same. Amy mentioned something about a party later in the week at Marissa Guidera's house.

"Her parents are out of town," she said. "Her sister's making Jell-O shots. I think. All the seniors will be there."

"I hate Marissa," Kari said. "I heard her sister had, like, three abortions."

"But you're still going, aren't you?" Gary asked.

"Of course. Do you think there'll be a list?"

"Fuck a list," Gary scoffed. I pretended to laugh.

"Are you going, Miles?" Amy asked me.

"Call him 'Retard,'" Gary corrected. "That's his name."

"Gary!" Kari slapped him on the shoulder.

"What? That's his name. He likes it."

I just sort of shrugged, chuckling.

"Well," Kari asked. "Are you going?"

I doubted very much that I would be on any list if there was one. "Maybe," I said. "I'll probably go. I don't know."

"Does Marissa have a pool?" Gary wanted to know. It took almost fifteen minutes for the girls to decide.

After dinner—the girls had salads, the boys had steak, only I could barely keep mine down—the four of us walked over to the movie theater. While they were getting popcorn I excused myself to the men's room and took two pills. They kicked in by the end of the previews and I nearly fell asleep during the movie, which was some stupid chick film about a group of ordinary suburban girls who wanted to be princesses and then found out that they actually were princesses, but in another dimension or something. Kari and Gary made out during the second half of the movie and I just sat there next to Amy, not even holding her hand. I couldn't tell whether I should make a move or not. I was scared. All I really wanted to do was get home and smoke a blunt. Chicks can be pretty awkward when they're not wasted, I guess. Or maybe it's just me. I can be pretty awkward.

~

Thomas Angel has started sleeping with me at night whenever I stay at my mom's. My sisters are jealous because they each want him in their bed at night. I could care less where the cat sleeps. He is kind of warm though and that's nice. He rubs up against my face in the mornings and does a little dance on my chest. I like having him curled up next to me okay, but sometimes his breath smells like dead things.

~

Do you know what I always HATED about school, besides everything? Scratch that. Let me start over. Do you know who I always hated? Besides all the teachers and coaches . . . I always hated the *oooooh-aaaawww* kids. You know the ones. All those dickheads who go *ooooooh* or *aaaawww* whenever anyone gets in trouble. You step the slightest bit out of line and you get an immediate chorus of moans. There they are, smirking and grinning. Or covering their mouths. It's disgusting. For as long as I can remember I've made it a point not to be a part of that crowd. I'm usually the one getting *ooooooh*'d at. It's always been like that.

The funny thing is, douchebags like that desperately need kids like me. It gives them an excuse to gloat and make a lot of noise. If nobody talks back to the teacher, a whole room full of jerks are stuck with their thumb in their butt, waiting for the bell to ring. Hanging on the edge of their seats, ready to pounce in case somebody farts or raises their hand the wrong way. I used to get *ooooooh*'d sometimes when I wasn't even trying to be disrespectful. Just for asking what I thought was a pretty reasonable question about whatever bullshit topic was at hand. Then, if you turn around and give those bastards the finger, you get put out by the teacher. And the *ooooooh*'s rise even higher. It's a vicious fucking circle. I've never wanted any part of it.

Another thing I always hated: when the kids at school, and it's usually the same kind of kids I already mentioned, when they catch you doing something and the teacher isn't around. They usually tell you something like, "You know you can't do that." What they actually mean is: You are not ALLOWED to do that or What you are doing is AGAINST THE RULES. I've already mentioned how literal I used to be about everything. Well this pet peeve is a holdout. I wish people would just keep their mouths shut. I CAN do whatever I want. Within the realm of human capability, that is. I mean I can't fly or shoot lasers out my eyes or anything gnarly and superhuman like that, but if I want to grab an extra rice pudding at the lunch line or forge a hall pass or whatever, then I'm gonna fucking do it. I may get a stern lecture or sent for a time-out or end up being *aaaawww*'d by a room full of assholes, but I CAN do it. I mean, it is physically possible to steal pudding. School rules aren't exactly the laws of gravity, you know.

~

The rain is coming down in buckets and I'm feeling pretty crummy. I can't skate and I'm sick of all my video games. They've been feeling more and more like a waste of time lately. Not that I have anything better to do. TV sucks at the moment and I've seen all the good movies at the store. There's nothing to do. Nada. So I call the Beaster Bunny, hoping he's picked up the nuggets he promised to spot me the last time we talked . . . He has!!! But he says he won't drive them over. When I ask him why, all he tells me is he doesn't feel like it. So I suit up for the rain.

I'm wearing my dad's old poncho from the seventies, which is covered in patches and stains, but it's the only suitably waterproof thing I own, except for my puffy-ass winter ski jacket and it's like ninety degrees outside, so that is way the fuck out of the picture. Since I don't want to get my shoes all waterlogged, I hop on my bike in bare feet. I start pedaling over to Robby's folks' house with thoughts of good herb on the brain. Robby agreed to spot me a half-ounce on the condition that I get rid of it by the end of the week. That's three days from now.

I can't see anything and by the time I'm out of my mom's neighborhood, Dad's poncho has already soaked through completely. My T-shirt is sticking to my skin. The water is rising around the base of my wheels, my feet. I wonder if the cicadas can swim. And what about the moles . . . As I'm crossing Northern Parkway, somebody leans on their horn. I stop my bike and flip them the bird, but their taillights have already disappeared in the storm. A minute later, as I'm cutting through Homeland, my tires skid out and I slide across the pavement. I land in a puddle. The entire inside of my leg is covered in a nasty concrete rash and I think the toenail on my big toe is coming off. There's a lot of blood. I sit in the road a few a seconds, feeling dirty and wet. Water runs past my ass cheeks, rushes right through my lax shorts. I cuss at myself. Cuss at the weather. The world . . . Sometimes I feel so low I could sit on a deck of cards and dangle my legs over the side . . . I get up and keep riding. You gotta keep forever going. If only because there's nothing else to do.

When I get to Robby's front door, he has somebody over, the potman I guess, and he won't let me in. He says I'm too wet. And bloody. Whatever, Robby. I wait outside for him to weigh the shit out and triple-bag it against the rain. It's really coming down now. I tell myself I won't thank him when he hands me the bag. But I do anyway. All the way home, I hate myself for it.

I ditch my bike in the garage and run upstairs, where I pinch a gram or so from the bag. I wrap it in cigarette cellophane and stow it in the cushions on my futon. I'm about to change my clothes before I head back out, but I realize they'll just get soaked anyway. I dash across the street in the rain. When I get to the old man's front door, I must look a complete mess. I ring the bell.

It takes a little while for him to answer the door, but I can hear him moving around in there. Bad joints, I figure. Unless he's hiding something . . .

When he finally opens up, I'm a little taken aback. He's wearing a set of old-timey pajamas. Like a dress, with a stocking cap and everything . . . He looks pretty surprised, too. I guess he wasn't expecting company. Not to mention someone as waterlogged and bloody as I am. But he lets me in anyway and scurries off somewhere to get me a towel, even though I tell him not to bother.

While I'm waiting in the front hall, I take the chance to scope out his decor. The front hall is laid out exactly the same as our front hall, except for the pictures. All over the walls, even way up high where he must have needed a ladder to get to, are rows and rows of framed posters and photographs, mostly black and white. It's pretty sweet actually. All we have is a lot of white space and few strategically placed prints of ducks and flowers and nautical maps and shit. You can tell Mister Reese didn't hire a decorator, like my mother always does. For some reason that seems pretty cool to me.

Mister Reese comes back down with a towel, plus gauze pads, tape, and peroxide for my legs. He shows me the first floor powder room, even though I already know where it is because our house has the exact same one. I thank him, shut the door behind me, flick on the lights. Wow. Clowns. Everywhere. Even a big poster on the ceiling. Like I'm in a nursery or something. It kinda-sorta freaks me out. I'm already thinking John Wayne Gacy or something. I clean up and dry off. I get some of my blood on the towel and feel bad. I hide it under the sink. I nervously picture the old man waiting outside with his ear to the door. I try not to wince when I clean out my big toe, which is starting to hurt pretty bad. I don't want him to hear me.

We go upstairs to his living room. More of the same. Pictures, I mean. Lots of them. And posters. And clowns. Plus all this random shit, like a mini totem pole and a samurai sword and a two-headed baby shark floating in a jar. And NO TELEVISION, I notice, at least not in the main hangout room . . . Mister Reese sits down in front of a coffee table, where there's a tray of milk and cookies set up. He must've been eating them when I rang the doorbell. A silence passes between us and I feel awkward. I wonder who's gonna make the first stab at small talk. I break first. I ask him for a cookie. He waves his hand over the tray like "Hey, help yourself, man" so I snatch one up and dunk it in the milk, but I'm kind of careless and my fingertips end up dipping slightly into his milk along with my cookie. I can't tell if he notices but I feel bad anyway. I look around for a distraction or a change of subject. I ask him about the pictures.

"Anarchists," he says. "Anarchists, clowns, magicians, musicians, monsters, and movie stars mostly."

I don't know what to say. All I can think of is, "Rad."

~

How far can a boy get on two hundred dollars? To Florida and then the Caribbean Sea? I guess not. Whenever I dream of running away it always strikes me as impossible. If only I lived back in the day when you could hop a freight train or a tramp steamer and set out into a world of opportunity. Even hitchhiking is supposedly illegal nowadays. Besides, I'm not into giving blow jobs.

One day I'll run off to the woods or an island. I'm sure of it. And things will be better there. I'll bounce through the trees like a naked ape, callous to insect bites and small wounds. Nature Boy they'll call me. And I'll be free . . . But for now I guess I better pay Robby back. And get him to spot me another half oz. Maybe a whole one this time . . .

~

Sometimes after my mother goes to bed, I come and tuck her in for the night. I leave a glass of water by her bedside or turn on the fan to deal with her hot flashes. Shit like that. Sometimes she wakes up and asks me to rub her feet. Her dogs are constantly sore from work. They are heavily calloused and kind of gross. I massage them even though I don't want to. I feel bad for her I guess. Once in a while I'll be standing by her bedside in the dark, giving those sore dogs a rubdown, and it will make me think of Jesus. You know, washing Simon Peter's feet. I don't know why, but that makes me feel better about myself.

I still wash my hands afterward though. Feet are gross.

~

I run into Mister Reese as he is going for one of his walks around the neighborhood. I join him and we get to talking and somehow it comes out how much I hate my sisters. "You don't hate them," he tells me.

"Yes. I do. They suck."

"Life is too short to spend on hate, kid."

"Yeah. I guess."

"You don't even know how to hate yet. You're too young. When you learn to hate, you'll know it. And you'll want to forget."

"But I get so pissed at them sometimes . . ."

"Well, that'll happen. With lots of people. Let it pass. They're just like you probably. At least some part of them is."

"But what about my dad? He sucks too."

"You don't hate him either, I bet. Hate is a strong feeling to have. Hate is absolute. Impenetrable. At least while it lasts."

"I guess you're right."

I sighed and kicked a pebble out in front of me.

Usually I hate being wrong, but this time it felt okay.

~

So . . . I spend yesterday afternoon tooling around on Jon's go-kart with him and Gary. Then we get picked up by Devin French and Anthony Kalista, sophomores at Jon and Gary's school. We're headed to Marissa Guidera's house party. The sophomores insist on getting high first and since I'm the only one holding anything, the burden falls on me. We smoke the last of my pot—the gram and a half I pinched from Mister Reese's bag—in the car on the way to the party.

When we get to Marissa's backyard—there *is* a swimming pool, even though nobody's in it—I find myself surrounded by a lot of people I don't know or barely know or only know by name. Jon and Gary spend half the night being initiated via beer bong by a group of incoming seniors who wear their resort-colored polo shirts with the collars turned up. They leave me out of it because I go to a different school than them, I guess. Thank god . . . People keep rubbing me on the top of my head. People keep asking me about my little sisters. It gets annoying. Joan Batton, whose older brother is now a famous reality show douchebag in Hollywood, gives me a big wet kiss directly on my winespot when she sees me. Our parents are friends and she is piss drunk and holding a beer bong, but still it was kind of nice . . . By midnight, Gary and Kari have gotten in a fight and Jon has already made out with three girls, including Amy. I don't care though. I never even try to talk to her. I only hug her for a second and she pecks me on the cheek when we first get there and then we don't speak for the rest of the night and it feels weird.

I end up shitfaced and hanging around the outskirts of the party until I come across a game of Truth or Dare that's going on near the deep end of the pool. I sit down on the patio and slide myself into the circle. Even though I kind of know or at least used to know a few of the people in the game, nobody ever calls on me. When it's finally my turn to ask truth or dare? I turn to Tracy Cottle and find myself asking a two-part question. "Part one," I say. "Toilet paper: Crumple or Fold?"

Tracy blushes a little. "Crumple," she says. "I guess. *I don't know.*" She puts her face in her hands and says, "Oh my god."

"Part two. Front-Wipe or Back?"

"I don't know," she squeaks. "You are gross."

Somebody jumps in and asks a new question. A minute later Tracy gets up and leaves the circle. The game dissolves pretty quickly after that. And I'm feeling very drunk.

I smoke a cigarette by myself, waiting for someone to come talk to me. Nobody comes. I walk out front and look at the numbers on the mailbox. Then I go inside to look for the house phone. I call Russian Stan and give him the address. It costs me thirty-five dollars to get home. Whatever. I wanted to leave. And the cops were probably on their way anyhow . . . Stan drops me off at my mother's. I slip inside and turn on the television. I can't sleep and I'm out of pills, so I drink Nyquil until it finally puts me out.

When I wake up this morning I have a bad hangover and no marijuana. I panic. I slip on a pair of pajama pants and a T-shirt. I walk outside and the sun burns me on the eyeballs. I think I'm going to faint, but I don't. There are a bunch of little neighborhood kids lying on top of the high-voltage boxes, like lizards in the sun. One of them looks up at me and sticks his tongue out. They ask where my sisters are and I shrug, keep walking.

When Mister Reese opens the door, he doesn't seem surprised to see me. He invites me inside. On the way upstairs, he tells me I smell like a brewery. "I feel like an outhouse," I tell him. He chuckles. He offers me a cup of tea. Apparently he was already making a pot when I rang. I tell him thank you and accept.

We drink our tea in virtual silence. I'm not sure how to ask him if he wants to get me high. I'm hoping he'll bring it up so I won't have to. I pray a silent prayer of thanks when he breaks out his pipe. It's a pretty nice one too—some kind of fancy dark wood, with a Sherlock Holmes–style shape to it. He doesn't pass it though. Instead he offers to let me use one of his backup pipes, a little corncob thingy. I've never smoked like that before, not sharing or passing the pipe, but both of us puffing away at the same time. It's kind of nice though. Civilized or something. It makes me feel old, but in a good way.

Somehow we end up talking about AA. I think he brings it up. I tell him how I used to go to Alateen after I got in trouble. He just sort of nods, looks down at his tea cup. He used to go to AA, he says. His second wife made him go. "It can get a little cornball at times," he tells me. "But it works for a lot of people." He's hitting the pipe when he says it.

"You hear some pretty crazy stories," I tell him, just trying to fill a gap in the conversation. "That's for sure."

"Ain't that the truth," he coughs. "All kind of desperate stories. Those rooms can be a regular soap opera," he says. "Days of Our Livers . . ."

I end up laughing and coughing until snot comes out my nose. And Mister Reese laughs too, just watching me . . . I think we are friends. Although I will continue to tax him and pinch from his bag when it comes to our business transactions.

~

Dropped loot off at Robby's today. I asked if he wanted to go tubing. He wasn't into it. He told me to call him later tonight and by then he would have re-upped on his stash. I went to my mom's and practiced old school–style streetplants on the sidewalk out front. A few minutes went by and Donald Diamond walked past me on the sidewalk. I think I saw him roll his eyes. I sneered at him, gave him a rat-face. He gave me the finger. I picked up my board and made like I was going to charge him down with it. But he didn't run away or even flinch. Shit. I threw my head back and pretended to laugh. I fake-laughed like that for what felt like forever. Time froze. I sort of hoped he would hit me or something, anything to break up the tension. He just stood there watching me like I was the light rail and he caught me veering off my tracks. I must've looked crazy. I stopped laughing and hopped on my board. As I was skating away I looked over my shoulder and watched him waddling into his house, probably confused. The entire exchange went poorly for ol' Retard.

Later on I stopped by Mister Reese's, hoping to get high. I talked up Robby's new stash, thinking it might get him excited to smoke. He just sort of shrugged. I guess he still has a bunch left over from Tuesday. He invited me in though. We went upstairs. It's amazing how much room this guy has all to himself. His house is exactly like ours, only we have four people and a cat. I wondered what he does when he's all alone. I would just go wild, I bet. Scream, jump on the couches, the tables, have food fights with the mirror . . . We made small talk and then Mister Reese put on a record. He has records everywhere. His cabinets are full of them. They sit against the walls in huge stacks. Some of them are hanging like pictures. This one was full of old-timey sounding hillbilly songs. I sat and listened a few minutes, hoping he'd break out the pipes. He didn't. Instead he closed his eyes. I couldn't tell if he was sleeping or not. I learned forward to see if he was snoring. I couldn't tell. I waited a minute. I cleared my throat. I told him I liked the music. I waited for him to respond. He didn't. I listened closely to this pretty old song about a man who was bound to hang. It was sad and spooky at the same time. It made me think of the music I'd been hearing around the neighborhood all summer. I decided to ask him about it. A smile spread across his face. He jumped up and winked at me. Then he scrambled upstairs. It was no joke, how spry he could be on those creaky old bones. Like a gray squirrel bolting up a telephone pole. He came back down with a dark wooden banjo strapped across his chest. He played along with the record, grinning from ear to ear.

I clapped my hands together. "So that was you all this time?" Stupid question.

"Yessiree," he nodded. "I've been hoping someone in the neighborhood would take notice. Even if it was just to complain. This place could use a little music," he said.

He opened the screen door and we went out onto the deck. I sat on the railing and watched him play. He looked happy. And COOL! Really, he did. He was totally jamming. I bobbed my head and pretended to dance. It made him smile.

After a while I thought of something. "What were you doing with that rat?" I asked. "The one you showed me out on the street? The one in the paper bag?"

"That was for Tickles," he told me. "That was Tickles's rat."

"Oh. Okay . . . Who's Tickles?"

"Tickles is a big fat snake," he said, still playing. "He lives upstairs. He eats one or two of those white rats every month."

"Really? I never met any, um, old . . ." I corrected myself. "Er . . . Older dudes that like snakes . . . Enough to own one, I mean."

"I don't really like him." He plucked a warbling little birdsong with his right hand. "I'm taking care of him for a friend. She can't keep him in her apartment . . . Actually I like rats better than snakes by a damn sight. It's kind of a moral dilemma."

"Okay," I said. "Can I see him?"

"I don't see why not. Come upstairs and I'll introduce you."

We went upstairs. The stairway was full of posters for magic acts. Against the back wall of what would be my bedroom if this was my mom's house, there was a huge aquarium made of sanded-down plywood and glass. There was a jungle of rocks and ferns inside and two big red heat lamps on top. I had to get up close to separate Tickles from his surroundings. He was HUGE. Five or six feet long. And FAT TOO! Like one long muscle covered in scales.

That must be what the twins saw Mister Reese carrying into his house, I realized. Tickles the snake. I wondered if he was lonely living in that tank. Mister Reese said I could pet him if I wanted, but I didn't. I just felt bad for him is all. And I wondered what he might look like with a set of tiny legs.

~

I was six years old the first time I learned what fucking is. We were at a family party. Someone's baptism or first communion or some shit. My mother had me dressed up in a little bow tie. She was showing me off to the adults. Looking back on it, she was probably drunk. She kept dragging me along behind her. My father told me to put my hands in my pockets so I wouldn't bite my nails or pick my nose in front of anyone important. I kept having to take them out to shake hands. I got bored of that scene pretty quickly. I slunk off toward the kids' quarters downstairs, where all my cousins were hanging out with their friends. I was the youngest at the party except my sisters who were practically babies, or at least that's how I saw them. I felt more aligned with the big kids myself. I wanted to belong.

The basement was dark like black velvet, except for the flicker and glow of the TV. Everyone was hunkered down together like kittens, all along the circular sofa and stretched out across the floor on cushions. At the bottom of the steps, I started to chirp my little "Hello!" But the whole room shushed me. So I just plopped down on the carpet and sat myself Indian-style, right up front by the screen.

Hulking across my cousins' television was a monstrous radioactive lizard-beast, a space alien with giant teeth. He lurched past a locker room shower and slammed a pretty yellow-haired lady up against a wall of metal gym lockers. His eyes were pitch black and hollow like an insect's, like deep tunnels leading nowhere. The poor lady screamed bloody murder as the monster thrust himself between her legs from behind. She was squirming and moaning and crying between deep exhausted breaths. The monster flicked his huge tongue at the camera. It was purple. I thought he was going to suck out her brain.

"What is he doing to her!?" I wanted to know.

"He's FUCKING her!" One of my cousin's friends shouted. They all told him to shush. But I had already heard the F-word before, although I didn't have a very firm grasp on its meaning. Not really. I just knew it was something real bad. All the cuss words rolled up into a nasty black ball, was about what I imagined. The monster ripped a claw down the blonde chick's back. She squealed as her skin peeled off in ribbons. I turned to my cousin Annie for an explanation.

"The aliens are trying to get that woman pregnant," she told me. "So she has a half-alien monster baby. That's how it works. Then they can use it to take over the planet . . . Um, maybe you shouldn't be watching this," she suggested, leaning forward to peek in my eyes. I rolled away from her and sat in the corner. After a while I got bored and went upstairs to look for my mom, but the damage had already been done. The next week at school, I was telling everybody about what I'd seen that lizard do.

Word spread to the teachers pretty quickly. It always did. Wild rumors were whipping around my pre-first classroom. Even the first graders were interested. All about spaceships and alien abductions and humongoid reptile-men raping pretty blonde teenagers in the shower. In other words, all about how babies were made. Parents were called. A conference was set up. The fifth grade science teacher had to come in and give us an impromptu lesson in rudimentary anatomy. A lot of mothers didn't want their sons hanging around with me after that. They told my parents so. My parents felt bad for me. I told them it didn't bother me. I still do.

~

Secret: Sometimes I'm tempted to leave my journal on a bench or someplace where strangers might find it and read what's inside and learn about me . . . But I'm also afraid my handwriting might be too messy and they'll throw the whole thing out without reading. Then I'll have wasted my time. And that scares me worse than almost anything. Wasting time . . . I know. It's sad.

~

Mister Reese used to be a magician, among other things. While we were smoking in his living room, I asked him about all the clowns and magicians hung on the walls and he told me he used to perform at parties and stuff and even went on tour with a carnival. I always dug magicians so I asked him to bust out some tricks. "I'll show you a trick," he told me. "Close your eyes."

I closed my eyes, but by accident I peeked.

"A little peeking is all right for this one," he said. He turned his hands over to show me they were empty. "But it demonstrates a lack of trust. That's all right too. Never trust a magician."

"Do the trick already."

"Close your eyes," he said. "Now try your damnedest not to picture an elephant."

"Hey!" My eyes were still pinched tight. "Fuck you. I just did picture an elephant."

"I know. You can't do it. That's the trick."

I opened my eyes. "That's lazy magic, dude. Not cool."

"The power of suggestion," he smiled, obviously pleased with himself. "Is strong magic."

"Whatever. Do something else."

He reached across the coffee table. He pulled a fluffy green nugget from behind my earlobe, then held it out in front of my face.

"Can I have it?" I asked, feeling hopeful.

He tossed the bud at my lap. I caught it.

"Now make Tickles disappear," I told him.

"I wish I could," he chuckled. "Make him disappear forever."

~

This afternoon I caught the MTA downtown to go skating. The inside of the bus smelled like cat piss. The tints were peeling off the windows and the back of my seat was covered in stab wounds. Foam stuffing was coming out the slashes and holes in stale yellow crumbs that looked like boogers. Everyone was sweating. There were too many people onboard for this kind of weather. The woman in front of me was having a nervous breakdown because her hair-weave fell out. She was holding it in her hands like a dead ferret, blubbering. People were laughing at her.

At a stop near North Avenue a man got on the bus with a chicken box and sat across from me. "Is that a skateboard?" he asked, pointing. I just nodded. It took him less than five seconds to get his box open and smear hot sauce all over his face. Chicken skin hanging from his moustache. Then he started to go on and on about terrorism.

I HATE IT when people complain about the terrorists. It's all anybody talks about anymore. They love to gossip about death. Terror just sits in the back of their minds like a demon, a vulture picking at their thoughts. They have to say something or they'll scream. And you can't turn on the television without hearing it either. The terror alert has reached blood orange! Demon red! Fucking purple, for chrissakes! Planes are going to pop out of the sky like fireworks! Decapitation! Chemical warfare! Nuclear jihad! Nobody's safe! We're all being watched! DC is gonna blow and knock over our poor city like a set of dominoes! Or radiation will catch the breeze like a child's kite and give the whole town cancer! Jesus, give it a rest already . . . It's so boring . . . Even if we *are* all about to die, we don't have to sit around talking about it, do we? Well this slob on the bus must've thought he could talk Death to death, the way he was running his mouth. Shit, he probably could've. Someone needs to give this guy his own talk show. *The Doom Hour with Donny* . . . And I had no choice but to sit there and listen to him. I was too much of a pussy to switch seats.

For one thing, I've heard it all before. Everyone on TV is an expert. The apocalypse is coming. The Last Days. Just look at the signs . . . Hurricanes, droughts, Ebola, Israel, cloning, the HIV, nuclear warheads, general terror . . . this guy even tried to bring the cicadas into his argument. Poor things . . .

"But they come every seventeen years, don't they?" I pointed out.

He wasn't listening. Civilization was about to freak out and die. We were all goners. And this guy had to vent his frustrations about it. His eyes were bugging out of his face. He looked scary. I didn't want to get on his bad side. I made sure he knew I agreed with him. "It's like, I try to sleep," I told him. "But I keep thinking about World War III." Which is kind of true anyhow.

"That's *good*," he said. I didn't see what was so good about it. But I kept my mouth shut.

I hopped off at Fayette Street. I was sick of listening to him. "Be careful on that skateboard," he called after me. "Those things are dangerous." Sure thing, buddy. Then, out the window as the bus was driving away, "And watch out for THE BOMB!" he yells. "Coming soon, man! ON . . . ITS . . . WAY!"

I ended up skating at the Holocaust Memorial. There are some decent stepped ledges there that are usually waxed up. The statue is in the middle: a giant bronze torch full of charred skeletons, screaming. It's pretty gnarly. A good place for photos. Eventually I got chased off by the fuzz. Fucking sk8 Nazis . . . So I rolled over to Water Street for a cheeseburger. On the way I passed an arabber's horsecart dragging around a bunch of rotting vegetables. He was a black dude with braids and he called out his produce in rhyme.

The horse pulling his cart looked totally exhausted. Spent. You could tell it wanted to go home. I stepped off the sidewalk to pet it on the nose and the horse snorted at me with its big-ass nostrils. I flinched. I thought it was going to bite my fingers off. The arabber chuckled when he saw this and worked me into his rhyme: "Apples, oranges, corn, tomatoes . . . Little boy scared to pet my horse on the nose . . . Apples, oranges, corn, tomatoes . . . Come get 'em quick before everything goes . . ."

I've got to admit, for a few seconds at least, I felt like a celebrity.

~

When I was younger, the walls of my bedroom used to be covered in beer and malt liquor promos, full of pretty blonde chicks playing volleyball or riding motorcycles in their bikinis. I'd get all these posters and cardboard cutouts from the guys who owned the liquor store on York Road where my mom went for her beer and lottery tickets. The guys there made me show them my report card each month and they'd give me something for each B that I got. Like a little reward for doing okay. So my walls were covered with skin. And that's how I liked it. At least for a while.

I say "for a while" because, even though the beer girls were WAY hot, the ads themselves were pretty corny and even kind of embarrassing. So as I got a little bit older, I stopped collecting new posters. I kept the old ones though. Mostly because I couldn't figure out what else to put on my walls. Right now, the posters are spread out between both houses. There are even some on the floor of the garage at the old place. From moving around so much, they've gotten all cracked and wrinkly, peeling and full of little holes.

I may decide to throw everything out and start high school fresh with clean walls. But I can't make up my mind. I can never make up my mind.

~

I woke up this morning with the powerful urge to play Cowboys and Indians or something childish like that, but instead I smoked a pipe and went over to visit old Mister Reese. We made tuna fish sandwiches in his kitchen and took them down to Robert E. Lee Park for a picnic. It was perfect outside, clear and warm but not too hot. From time to time a misty rain fell through the sunshine like diamonds and evaporated against our skin. We stood by Lake Roland and watched the water spill over the dam. I kept trying to skip stones off the water but they all broke the surface like *plop!* and sank right to the bottom.

Mister Reese took a deep breath and patted himself on the stomach. "Hell of a day for the race," he declared, staring out over the lake.

"What race?" I asked. Preakness had already come and gone a while back.

"The human race, Miles. Hell of a day for the human race."

"Oh."

Somehow we began talking about death. He told me about his second wife. She passed away in a hospice. Mister Reese didn't like the place. "It was foul," he said. "Institutional. The lobby smelled like a bedpan." He shuddered. "And she couldn't talk in the end. Just growl like a dog. And make monster-movie sounds. She wrote on a notepad. Sad things. Scary things. Paranoia can set in pretty easy once you get that close to the end. She thought the nurses were stealing from her. Keeping her locked up at night . . . I saved some of her scribbles. I don't know why though. I'll never read them." He skipped a stone out over the lake. It bounced three or four times before falling in. "Maybe they'd make a good coffee table book," he laughed to himself. "All those scribbles. Oh, stop me. I'm terrible."

I asked him if he was scared of death. "No," he coughed. "I'm not scared of death. I'm scared I might live on forever without getting any younger. That's what's got me shaky."

I told him I thought I would like to live forever. I told him I thought time was very precious.

"Time, huh?" He took out his false teeth and wiped them on his shirtsleeve. His voice sounded different without any teeth. His mouth looked like a worn-out asshole. "Time is precious, you say.

But how do you know it's not working against you? Maybe time is not a gift. Maybe time is your enemy. A precious little vampire," he said, taking a pause to consider something. "Or maybe not. All I know is that it's good to be young. Youth is more precious than time. Keep a youthful head on your shoulders and anything might happen. Let yourself get old and there's only one thing that *will* happen . . . WHEN YOU'RE GREEN YOU GROW, WHEN YOU'RE RIPE YOU ROT . . . Write that down. It sounds like a cliché and it is, but it's also good advice."

I was staring at my reflection in the lake. "I will," I said. But I doubt he believed me.

Then we talked about how we wanted our bodies taken care of after we were gone. I said I wanted to be mummified and put on display in a museum or a circus. Mister Reese just complained about how expensive funerals had gotten. He said he wants to forgo burial costs altogether. He said he wants someone to throw his body out past the tides when it's time for him to go.

"When my earthly trials are over," the old man said, tossing a pebble out over the dam. "Cast my body out in the sea. You can save on the undertaker bill. Let the money float with me."

Everything was quiet for a moment, except the sound of falling water.

"Are you ever really afraid that you might live on forever without getting any younger?" I asked, not knowing what else to say.

"Heck no." He slipped his teeth back in his mouth and chomped them in place, like a horse. He looks a lot better with teeth. "Don't they teach science at that school of yours?"

I just kind of shrugged.

"No way," he went on. "But I used to think I might could be a god. As I get older and fouler, my bowels keep reminding me otherwise."

I let the last part of my tuna sandwich drop from my lips into the water. I watched as a scaly orange carp popped up to gobble it off the surface.

"That makes sense," I agreed, after thinking about it a minute . . . I couldn't imagine god having to take a shit. And what would that shit look like, anyway?

~

Thomas Angel woke me up this morning. He was standing on my bare chest, sniffing at my breath when I woke up panicked from a dream. Thomas Angel slipped off and dragged his claws down my rib cage. The blood came fast, like it had been waiting there just beneath my skin for an opportunity to escape. When I saw it, I reacted. I couldn't help it. I threw the cat into the air. He whined like a smoke alarm as he sailed across the room. He hit the wall with a thud.

Kelly and Katie came running upstairs when they heard the noise. They popped my lock and burst in through the door. Thomas Angel was trembling in the corner. The girls called me a "monster." They took the cat away from me. They petted his coat and kissed him. They whispered baby talk into his ears.

Now my sisters aren't speaking to me, whatever that means. But I don't really mind. I feel a little sorry for Thomas Angel though. I wish I could apologize. I wish he could understand me.

~

Secret: I will be forever shocked and amazed at my body's infinite ability to produce things like boogers and wax and dead skin. When will the supply ever run thin?

And sometimes I make turds so big I can't believe that it was I who created them. I'm filled with awe. Their size, their shape . . . It shocks me to think I could have been lugging something like that around with me all day. And in my belly no less! Times like these I stand over the toilet and take a short pause before flushing, then watch as those whales get sucked down into the deep where they'll disappear from my life forever.

Goodbye, turds.

~

I knocked on Mister Reese's door today and waited, but nobody answered. The door was unlocked and I went inside. Upstairs, I found Mister Reese with his feet up, wearing a bathrobe and a black top hat, with a digital thermometer sticking out the corner of his mouth like a cigar. The same black woman I had seen from before was sitting next to him, taking his blood pressure with one of those pumps that wraps around your arm. Her sweatpants were ratty and covered in bleach stains I noticed, but she was wearing full makeup. Her eyelids were painted blue, the color of a swimming pool. It was kind of sexy in a weird way. When she saw me at the top of the stairs, she licked the fuzz over her lip with her tongue.

She poked Mister Reese on the ear with a long purple fingernail. "I hadn't an inkling that you were in the possession of such handsome young friends, old man," she said, sounding all mock-proper and Caucasian. Mister Reese just shrugged.

"I didn't know you had a nurse, Mister Reese," I told him, taking a seat. "That's, uh . . . something."

"She is not my nurse," Mister Reese mumbled around his thermometer.

"I'm the closest thing you got to a nurse at the moment." She put away the blood pressure machine and took the thermometer from his lips. She barely glanced at it before tossing it in her bag. "People can be so ungrateful sometimes," she said to herself. Then, to the old man, "Why don't you introduce me to your little friend already?"

"*Nurse* Brown, this is Miles. Miles, Nurse Brown."

She leaned forward and kissed me on the cheek. Her lips were soft and wet, like they were covered in Vaseline. "I ain't no real nurse," she said, shaking her head. "Call me Diamontay."

"Dimetapp?"

"Diamontay, honey. Say it like Diamond—minus the *d*, plus the *tay* . . ."

"Minus the *d*, plus the *tay*," I repeated.

"Oooh, and he's smart too. What are you doing hanging around this old head case for?"

"Go check on your snake already, why don't you?" Mister Reese cut her off. "I think I saw him trying to swallow himself earlier."

"I sure he's fine as long as you fed him," Diamontay said. "Me and Tickles organize our own visiting schedule, thank you. And guess what? It's not even a bit of your business."

"Tickles is your snake?" I asked. Somehow it didn't fit that this woman would be someone who keeps reptiles.

"Tickles is my *baby*," she said, hugging her purse like she was holding an infant.

"Some baby," Mister Reese snorted. "I have nightmares about that thing."

"Oh shut your mouth. He's lying, Miles. Don't even listen to him. He secretly loves having my Mister Tickles around. He enjoys the company."

"Oh, that's rich . . . But you might be right. Frankly, I prefer the company of a snake to most humans. Who doesn't? That Tickles is quite the conversationalist."

"Very funny. Don't let him hear you say that or you just might wake up from your catnap with a snakeskin necktie one of these days."

"That's what I keep him around for." Mister Reese produced a pipe from somewhere inside his robe and lit it. "Death by snake is a personal fantasy of mine. Very adventurous, don't you think?"

"I'm sorry, Miss Diamontay," I heard my little voice saying. "But if you don't mind me asking, why did you give Tickles up? Seeing how much you love him, I mean."

"Had to. I live with my sister and her husband and they just had a baby. They don't want the snake around the child, which I understand . . . They don't want no kind of pet to tell you the truth, Miles. They don't want that little boy having to confront death too early. And they're afraid that if the kid has a pet, that pet might die eventually, and the boy will have to deal with that shit."

"It will die," Mister Reese chimed in. "Eventually."

"Oh don't you be such a pessimist . . . I just as soon leave Tickles over here since I have to come around anyway. That way I can still come see him."

"But you aren't Mister Reese's nurse?" I was surprised to find myself asking all these questions so easily. Normally I'm kind of shy about meeting new people.

"Not technically. I'm not certified or anything. But I do the job. Check his vitals, you know. Do things around the house."

"She checks to see if I'm still breathing," said Mister Reese.

"Excuse me for asking, but how did you two meet?"

"I found her in the paper," he started. "I was looking for somebody to come over a few times a week. I was afraid I'd drop dead and nobody'd notice until I started stinking up the joint."

"Oh."

"And Diamontay here had an ad in the classifieds. For nanny services."

"I was looking to drive a few children to the pool is all," Diamontay said, rooting through her purse. "I had no idea what I was getting myself into. Did I, you old coot?"

Mister Reese flicked his top hat back onto the crown of his head and coughed a cloud of blue smoke in the air. "Not even the vaguest notion," he wheezed, shaking his head as Diamontay reached up to pat him on the back.

"You two are good for each other," I said. "You help each other out."

"I needed her for a reefer connection, until you came along," Mister Reese said. "Now I can't get rid of her." His eyes were watery from coughing and laughing. He looked pathetic, but cute. You could tell he was only joking, even though it was probably true. You could tell they cared about each other.

"I'm just praying the old bastard puts me in his will," Diamontay said. "That's the only reason I'm still around . . ."

"Mister Reese told me he wanted someone to throw all his savings out into the ocean when he dies," I told her, glad to be able to contribute something to the conversation.

"That's the kind of fool thing he *would* say." Diamontay reached over and snatched the pipe from Mister Reese's hands. "Smoking too much of that stuff," she said, striking a flame with her Bic. "Throw his money in the ocean, sheeee-it . . ."

Mister Reese leaned forward and slapped me on the knee. "She's only angry because she can't swim well enough to come after me," he joked. "She doesn't have it in her genes."

"We'll see how good *you* swim the next time you need me to

help you out of that bathtub, old man," Diamontay countered. And it went on like this into the afternoon, with me high and grinning and soaking it all in like a once-dry teabag bobbing in warm water.

~

I had a dream and in the dream I was sleeping nude in bed while a ceiling fan blew a cool breeze down against my skin and gave me goosebumps. There was a green night-light glowing on the wall near the bed I was lying in. It was shaped like a butterfly. Or a moth. I rolled over onto my stomach and stretched out my arms. I flapped them like wings against the mattress. I could feel something odd in the fabric. I probed it with the index finger of my left hand. A hole. Like a bellybutton. It was moist and warm inside. My fingers were drawn in deeper and deeper until I could feel something wiggling inside, wanting to get out. I started to panic. The mattress was covered in all these weird little recesses and there were moles scurrying out of them, on the bed all around me and on top of me. In fact, there had never been any ceiling fan at all. The cool ticklish feeling had been the pitter-patter of their tiny feet on my skin. And the longer I looked at these moles, I realized that they weren't normal moles at all but sleek, grinning, cartoon moles. They appeared to be running away from something, something beneath me, deep inside the mattress. That's when I began to hear the buzzing and feel a dense rumble below . . . Millions of red-eyed locusts stormed up from the bowels of my mattress, blasting the cartoon moles up into space and smothering me in a cloud of wings. I covered my mouth with my hands. I tried to think happy thoughts.

When all was said and done, I lay perfectly still on the pock-marked bed, waiting for the insects to rain their dry, spent exoskeletons down on top of me like confetti.

And then I woke up.

I went downstairs for a drink of water and found Thomas Angel in the kitchen, beating the crap out of a dead cicada. He purred when he saw me. I purred back.

~

Katie and Kelly have noticed me strolling around the neighborhood with my new friend and of course they're giving me shit for it. They still think Mister Reese is a serial killer or something, even though I told them he wasn't. They'd rather pretend that me and the old man are dating. Kelly called me his "trophy wife." I'll bet they tell Ashley Vidal all about it.

But fuck it. Mister Reese is my friend. Stupid bitches.

They've already got my mom in a panic. Last night around dinnertime I came home from lighting firecrackers on Gary's roof to find her sitting alone in the dark. All I could see was the orange tip of her cigarette, but I could already tell she'd been drinking. I could just tell.

"Miles, we need to talk," she said, trying to sound firm but breaking down entirely instead. She had heard that I was involved with a pedophile, she said.

"Where did you hear that?" I asked her, trying to stay calm.

She told me that she couldn't possibly reveal her sources but not to go after my sisters about it anyway. I swore I wouldn't lay a hand on either of those little bitches.

I tried to comfort her at first. I went over and sat on the arm of her chair. I gave her a hug. "I swear to Jesus, Mom," I told her. "I'm fine. He's just this weird old dude I hang out with. He's funny. He does magic. He's been teaching me songs on the banjo. For free."

Then she started bawling again, even harder now than before, as if I had confirmed something.

I couldn't take it. I hate seeing her cry. It pisses me off.

"Are you dead fucking serious with that shit!?" I snapped. "You think I suck old man dick!?!"

I stood up and stomped over to the light switch. I flicked on the lights. Mom squinted and covered her face like a vampire. She looked pretty bad. Her eyeballs were full of red veins and her face was wet. She had circles under her eyes. I hated to yell at her. But I did anyway.

I yelled at her for a while. Then we talked. Eventually she came around to see that nothing sinister was going on between me and our neighbor or me and anyone else for that matter. She said she would try to learn to trust my judgment sometimes and to not always assume the worst. And I think she really meant it this time. I think.

But, man, do I hate my little sisters.

~

The thing is, besides scrapple and eggs over light, my favorite breakfast food has always been a toasted English muffin, dripping with melted butter and honey. I enjoy them this way, with the honey. In fact, I have always thought honey was better than sugar. More natural or whatever. What do I know though? Probably everything is natural. If it exists, it must come from some kind of nature, right?

But today I woke up late on the couch at my mother's where I had passed out watching Shark Week on Animal Planet. After picking my butt for a minute or two, I stretched and headed upstairs to make my second favorite breakfast in the world, only as I was waiting for the honey to crawl down the inside of its plastic bear-shaped container, something happened inside my brain. I started thinking about where honey comes from. The bees. Not that I had been clueless about honey coming from beehives before today, but I had never put any deep thought to the matter is all.

It's really gross. Bees themselves are gross insects and poisonous too. But how exactly do they make the honey? It's not like they have farms and factories. Or tools or whatever. Does it come out of their butts? All that sweet, gooey honey the byproduct of millions of little bee butts? Is it sweet because they eat flowers all day? Maybe it's some kind of fluid leftover from constant intercourse with the queen bee? Even if it just comes from the wax in the hive somehow, how do they make the wax?

No, there was no getting around it.

In one way or another, the honey comes directly from the bees.

So I put the little bear back in his cupboard and used brown sugar instead, which melted into the nooks and crannies of my English muffin and turned it into some kind of foul caramelized sweet-tooth biscuit. I threw it off the balcony after one bite, figuring the birds would probably like it.

But now I can't eat honey anymore and I feel weird about it. I feel like a pussy. Would a caveman turn down honey when he discovered that it was made by insects? Fuck no! He'd be happy as a caveman on a belly full of honey. I should learn from this somehow, I think, but what should I learn? Maybe I'll talk it over with Mister Reese . . .

~

Mister Reese was asleep when I swung by his house this afternoon, but Diamontay let me in anyway. She was wearing a skimpy tank top and had Tickles the snake with her when she opened the door. He was twisted around her torso like it was a deep brown tree trunk, whispering into her ear. She petted Tickles on the forehead and he stuck out his tongue.

Diamontay led me out back to the deck where we sipped mint

tea and read fashion magazines while Motown hits drifted from the portable speaker she had hooked up to her iPod. Diamontay told me a story about an old homeless man she once knew, a junkie named Sky King who fell off the roof of a building she used to live in. Sky King, like a miracle, survived the fall with only minor bruises and fractures to the left side of his body, for which he was given painkillers. Delighted to have discovered what seemed like an excellent new RX connection, Sky King tried the stunt two more times and ended up in Sheppard Pratt, where he was diagnosed as a severe manic depressive and put on suicide watch. When he got out of the loony bin, he was clean for a day. And that was the day he got his nickname, Sky King. Then he started jumping off buildings again. It was a sad story, but funny the way she told it.

After a while, Diamontay asked me if I would hold the snake while she went in to check on Mister Reese. I wasn't sure if I wanted to or not, but I liked Diamontay and I didn't want to seem rude. Or look like a scaredy-cat for that matter. So I said okay.

She draped Tickles over my shoulders. He coiled his spine around my left forearm all the way up to my shoulder, then wrapped himself around my neck. A heavy bastard, he was. Diamontay went inside and left me with the snake. He kept moving around, climbing all over the chair and curling around my body, wrapping me up until it was a little disorienting trying to figure out which part of his body was which. So I quit trying. I gave myself up to the beast and slurped tea.

Tickles's skin was smooth and I trusted him. His wide jaw looked like it was frozen in a permanent close-mouthed smile. I closed my eyes for a minute or two and it was nice. I could feel him on me, moving, but the rest of the world was black. When I opened my eyes again, Tickles had stretched himself down toward my lap. He was probing my tea cup with his tongue, which was forked and trembling. He took a sip. I was glad. I wanted him to.

"I think he likes you, buddy," Diamontay said when she came out.

"We're old friends," I nodded, and gave Tickles a wink.

~

Walking with Mister Reese, hands in my pockets, birds in the sky, dead bugs breaking to pieces under my feet. The old man is carrying a big walking stick. I decide to ask him about the war.

"Were you in the war?" I ask. "My grandfather was in the war, but I didn't know him or anything . . . Maybe you two knew each other, huh?"

"Everyone was in the war," he says. "It was a big war."

"Oh. Yeah, I guess so . . . Were you, um, like the funnyman of your unit. You know, being a magician and all."

"Awww fuck," he goes. "I don't know. I guess I might have told a few jokes. People tend to tell jokes when they're scared as shit for their lives."

"Tell me a joke then . . . A war joke or whatever."

"A war joke?"

"Yeah. Like a joke you might have told or heard during the war. To keep up morale and stuff like that."

"I don't know, Miles. It really wasn't all that funny of a war."

"Come on, you old wuss. Please . . ."

"Okay," he said. His eyes looked thoughtful, like he was trying to make one up on the spot. After a minute or so he looked at me and said, "Knock, knock."

"All right," I said. "Who's there?"

"Francis."

"Francis who?"

"France is over there getting raped in the ass by Germany," he said, deadpan as all fuck.

"That's, um, not that funny."

Mister Reese shook his head. "I told you it wasn't," he reminded me.

And, dude, you know what, he was right.

~

I have always wanted to be blood brothers with somebody, like in Tom Sawyer and shit. But I can't ever seem to find anyone to be blood brothers with me. How do you ask somebody? What if they say no?

I think I might be getting too old for it anyway. Unless I somehow join the mafia or something. Besides, I imagine it's pretty unsafe in this day and age, what with the HIV and all that. So FUCK blood brotherhood for now, I guess. Until they find a cure, I'll keep my blood to myself, thank you very much.

Unless you want to share with me?

~

My parents have been fighting a lot lately. With each other. Over the phone. I think it has something to do with the fact that the renovations at the old crib are now complete. I think they might be selling pretty soon. Money tends to make people tense, I've noticed. And being tense makes them angry. And angry people fight.

My folks used to fight like vicious dogs when they were still living together, but now that they're apart again, I haven't had to see it in a while. I remember the last time I saw them really go at it in person. They were only very recently separated again. John was over and we came in to find them in a standoff. My mom was holding a small stool over her head and my dad was holding a pot of steaming water. John and I were ushered off the doorstep by Miss Sandy Diamond and taken to her house where my sisters were already waiting (in tears) with that douchebag Donald, who was trying all feeble to comfort them by showing them a book about dinosaurs. Fucking dinosaurs! I thought. At a time like this! John and me ran upstairs and ate a shitload of cookies while watching my mother's front door from Donald's window. After a minute, the fight spilled outside and we could hear my mother shrieking like a dolphin as she threw her wedding ring at the storm drain. It didn't go down at first. She charged over, stumbling, and kept stubbing her toe as she tried to kick it down the drain. Meanwhile my father was standing ten feet behind her, pointing, calling her names like a child.

When the police showed up, I grabbed John and my sisters and led them down to the basement under the pretense of a major video game session. Donald was upstairs helping his mother prepare a platter of kosher meats and cheeses for the occasion. Instead, I snuck everybody out the garage door and we high-tailed it through a secret hole in the neighborhood fence, then split over to Gary's and then to the country club where we played Sharks and Minnows in the deep end until it was dusky and the mosquitoes were coming out and our limbs had practically fallen off they were so tired from swimming. All that was left to do after that was invade the snack bar, where we ordered a tremendous feast on Gary's folks' account and gluttonized ourselves in the dying sun. We were happy then and felt about a million miles away.

And, you know what, for a moment there, I felt like a hero. But I never let anyone know until now.

~

Guess what, Journal? I can call you that, can't I? I mean we are on a first-name basis at this point, aren't we? Well, Journal, I've got a bone to pick with you: I sit here telling you all about my life and my family and my most intimate secrets and you give me nothing in return. It's like you don't trust me. I'm too stupid to understand your situation, is that it? Or what? You don't have any skeletons in your closet, huh? Your shit don't stink? Dead-fucking-serious, I think you're hiding something. Something dark, something scary . . . And I'll get to the bottom of it, whatever it is . . .

Nah, I'm just playing with you, baby . . . you're cool.

~

The other night, me and a bunch of other dudes slept over at John's house. We snuck out to party with his neighbor, this chick in the grade above us at Dulaney. She had some friends over. A few of them were hot. I ended up on the couch talking to one of the semi-hot ones. Her name was Kelsey. I was telling her all about those crystal skulls they found in Latin America. She seemed pretty interested. Eventually I got up to use the bathroom. While I was peeing I realized I had to vomit. I did it all neat in the toilet bowl and flushed. Then I gargled mouthwash for thirty seconds. When I came back out I found Kelsey right where I'd left her, only now she was sucking face with Blake Rogers. So I just kept drinking.

When we got back to John's we turned on the most recent *Terminator* flick and me and Stephen Kimble got everyone high. I don't remember anything after that, until later when I woke up to overhear John giving a whole speech about how hot my sisters were getting. He must've thought I was still asleep. I kept my eyes shut and listened. Everyone agreed about wanting to fuck them. Tommy Nesbitt even went so far as to say that I wouldn't do anything about it if one of them did happen to fuck my sisters. Somebody else corrected him. "WHEN we fuck them," they said. I could hear their laughter as I fell back to sleep and the whole terrible conversation drifted away like it had been a dream.

When I woke up in the morning, I went to the bathroom for a piss. Standing in front of the mirror, I saw my friends had trolled me. I was covered in black marker. There were crude penises drawn all over my face and across my chest was scrawled a mathematical equation. RETARD + LIFE = SUCKFEST, was what it said.

I was angry, but I pretended not to be.

I don't know, maybe it was funny.

All my so-called friends were laughing like hyenas over breakfast. Even John's mother had a chuckle on me. So, right there at the table, I laughed along with them.

Although I couldn't be sure why I was laughing and I felt bad about it afterward.

~

Thomas Angel murdered a mole today and delivered the carcass to our doorstep. I forgave him for it, but I'm nervous for the rest of the moles. Are they in danger now that he has discovered their colony? Should I help them relocate? Dig them up and transport them somewhere safer? Where is safer?

~

Mister Reese agreed to drive me out to Dulaney Valley so I could skate this drainage ditch on Pot Springs. He said he'd hang around and watch until I wanted to leave, which was real swell of him since I can't imagine anyone wanting to sweat their balls off all afternoon in a storm sewer just to see me skate . . . Anyhow, on the way there we found ourselves at a stoplight in Towson where I saw a woman hunched on the sidewalk. Despite the heat, she was wearing a full sweatsuit. It was fire-engine red and covered in stains and so tight that it clung to her bones. Real haggard-looking. Her hair hung down in clumps, not unlike the feces-caked strands that often dangle from the backside of long-haired dogs. This woman most definitely appeared to be homeless. She was even holding a sign she had made out of cardboard. As the light changed I craned my neck to read the sign, but it was completely blank. Nothing. Nada. Not a single word.

I considered the possible meanings behind this woman's blank sign. Maybe she was trying to indicate that she was illiterate as well as homeless and that those of us in traffic should have extra pity on her because of this. Maybe it was some kind of statement about the silence of poverty or the futility of signs. Or maybe she was just waiting for somebody to let her hold a pen . . . I thought of asking Mister Reese about it, but then I stopped myself. I was embarrassed. I felt foolish for wanting to ask him and I thought he would probably think I was foolish for asking . . . I mean, I can't expect him to explain EVERYTHING . . .

~

Yesterday evening, Katie and Kelly had a slumber party at my dad's place and we ordered pizzas for dinner. After dinner the girls asked me to play Hide and Go Seek Flashlight Tag with them in the graveyard on Homeland Avenue, just outside the gates of my father's community. I got really high before playing. That might have been a mistake.

Ashley Vidal was sleeping over along with a couple of the girls' other, less important friends. I pictured myself discovering her curled up all alone behind some gnarly tombstone or mausoleum, terrified but excited as heat lightning streaked the sky and the beam of my flashlight hit her on the chest, taking her out of the game and into my arms where she would feel safe and maybe want to French kiss . . . Silly, right?

Instead I ended up hopeless, lost in the rows and rows of marble blocks. I was trying to guide myself by the light of the half-moon instead of the flashlight so as not to give away my location, all the while being eaten alive by aggressive-as-fuck mosquitos. Nevermind the bugs. I kept bumping into stuff, stepping on dead bouquets, tripping over plaques at my feet. Playing the game in bare feet had been another big mistake. I must have already stubbed my big toe three or four times by this point, one time splitting the nail where I'd already busted it in my latest bicycle accident. I could see the girls' flashlights dancing like ghosts in the distance.

After what seemed like forever but was probably no more than twenty minutes, I decided I better sit down for a rest and try to get a better hold on the situation. I found an inviting little grave and planted my ass right on top. I took out a cigarette and decided to risk a smoke, even though I feared it might give away my location. I really wanted one but no way was I gonna be the first one caught and become IT. My sister's poor friend Sarah was currently IT, after losing a round of One Potato, Two Potato. If I ended up being IT, the whole night would be miserable. I'd probably suck at finding the others, which meant we could either be out here all night getting eaten alive or everyone would give up and go home to make fun of me for sucking at life. I might never get to see Ashley Vidal in her pajamas or possibly even play Truth or Dare. I cupped the tip of my smoke in my hand and walked as I smoked so the fumes would disperse in the air behind me and would be less likely to give me away.

The graveyard at night was a little bit eerie, to be honest. Occasionally I would hear the girls in the darkness around me, a burst of laughter or a shriek as they made their way down the rows. The sound of their voices sent shivers up my neck . . . At one point I came face to face with a stray cat, perched on top of a thick granite cross. The animal freaked me out a little, his eyes. He hissed at me, then evaporated on the spot . . . And there were hordes of tiny bats clipping the sky above my head. Do all graveyards have bats? Are they some kind of prerequisite? These bats were strictly decoration, I guess. They were doing very little to control the mosquito population . . . At one point I even saw what I took for an owl gliding across the light of the moon. It was enormous! As big as a human from wing to wing! I felt wild inside when I saw it! I imagined myself riding the back of the tremendous owl, cold air rushing past my face, fists gripped around monster-size quills as the beast bore me toward the moon . . .

And just then I was caught in the center of a white spotlight, like someone naked in a dream . . .

That little bitch Sarah had found me. Now I was IT. My heart sank.

I helped her round everyone up and we started all over again. I leaned my forehead against the cool outer wall of a large crypt and began counting one banana, two banana, three banana . . . all the way to a hundred. At first I could hear the girls whispering behind me. After they scattered, there was nothing but the sound of crickets and the occasional flap of low-flying bat wings. I was all alone. On the hunt. I decided to stop counting at around eighty banana and charged off into the darkness.

The night looked even darker now that I had to search through it. And the graveyard seemed more empty. I searched and searched, but I couldn't find a soul. My calves began to burn. I was sweating. The sweat attracted more bugs. They landed on me and fed off my skin. I was going in circles. I had lost all concept of time. I felt like I had been IT my whole life. I was becoming desperate. Where the fuck were those girls hiding?

At about this time, during the heat of my despair, I stepped on a fresh-picked rose at the foot of a grave. A very large thorn lodged itself in my heel. I sat down and perused the wound with my flashlight. It was more like a railroad spike than a normal-sized thorn. And it was in there pretty deep. Bleeding. With extreme caution I set about trying to pull the thorn from my foot. I didn't want it to break off inside me. But it did. It broke off inside me.

As I sat there bleeding in the grass, surrounded by the buried dead, it occurred to me that I hadn't seen the beam of another flashlight, not even once, ever since I had become IT. Come to think of it, I hadn't heard any voices or footfalls either. I was the only living person in the whole graveyard. I was sure of it. The twins and their little friends had ditched me.

I found my way to the road and limped back home, tired and bloody. I considered hopping the fence to the pool and washing myself off in the chlorine, but I decided against it. I wanted my little sisters to see the condition I was in when I came home to find them all snug in front of the television eating leftover pizza. I wanted them to feel guilty. I was livid. I meant to bitch them out, make them cry, ruin their little slumber party. And Ashley Vidal too. Fuck her for going along with them. In fact, fuck everybody. Fuck the world . . . That's about how I felt inside.

But when I got there, it was a different story altogether. I could see my sisters through the basement door. I had been right. They were all snugged out in their PJ's, on cushions in front of the flat screen, giving each other French braids and eating cold pizza. They were giggling and talking over one another, probably making fun of me, but I didn't want to bitch them out anymore. They looked happy. Besides, I didn't want to let them know they had gotten to me, gotten under my skin. I was too proud.

And they were only having fun, right? Why would I want to ruin their evening over a little joke? What kind of monster would that make me? How would I look? How would it make me feel?

So I left my herb inside to avoid seeing them and set off in the direction of Charles Street and our old house. With each step I took, I could feel the thorn climbing deeper and deeper into my foot. It hurt, but that didn't bother me. I got used to the thorn. By the time I got to the end of Homeland Avenue, I felt almost as if I deserved it somehow. The thorn was my cross to bear, like Jesus. That seemed like a cool idea at the time. I chain-smoked the whole distance and by the time I stumbled in the heavy old door, my throat was sore and my mouth tasted like garbage. But I felt good in a weird way. Relieved. I curled up beneath an oilcloth on the couch in our sunporch, where I used to watch Saturday morning cartoons when I was little. Just before drifting off to sleep, I stuck my thumb in my mouth like a baby. It tasted like cigarettes and sweat and cemetery filth. It nearly made me hurl. But I didn't hurl. I smiled and started to say a prayer in my head. For everyone I know. Even for some people I don't know, like those kids in Africa with the flies on their faces and stuff. And I fell asleep praying for the world and saying thank you. How about that? Weird, right?

~

Last summer I got into this fight with my sisters. It doesn't matter what the fight was about—something stupid—but the point is we got into a fight. As usual, the fight spread like a germ and soon I was fighting with my mother too. We were yelling and screaming at each other. I broke a small television on the kitchen floor. And the television cracked a tile when it fell. My mother called my father for help and he came over.

After about twenty-four hours, the whole thing blew over and my sisters apologized to me through the door and I said I'm sorry too. I was pretty embarrassed. I can't decide whether it's better to be ashamed of your flaws and mistakes or to just accept them openly. I wonder if it's possible to do both.

~

Mister Reese complains that the movies are fake because no one ever finishes their drink before leaving a restaurant. "Where are you gonna see somebody order and pay for a cocktail and then get up and leave it without finishing?" he says. "Only in Hollywood."

I only nod when he says this and store it in my memory for later. I don't spend enough time in bars to know what he is talking about. I'm too young. Although I have been able to figure out that most people are cheap and greedy when they get a chance to be . . . But on the other hand, they're also wasteful . . .

~

One nice thing is that regardless of whether people like me or not when I start school next month, I am pretty sure that Mister Reese will be my friend. Maybe he would be my friend even if I couldn't score him any more reefer for some reason. I would be his friend probably even if I wasn't pinching from the bags . . .

Another nice thing is peanut butter and jelly sandwiches out of a lunch box.

One more is pit beef during summer.

And snowballs.

~

I wake up and hit the pool. Ashley Vidal is there, wearing headphones and lying on her stomach. My sisters are nowhere in sight. I sit down next to her, but she doesn't seem to notice. Maybe she's asleep. With her sunglasses on, I can't tell. I pretend to flip through a comic book, but really I watch her out the corner of my eye.

And I want to talk to her.

And nothing happens.

~

The closer it gets to the end of the summer, the more jealous I grow of Thomas Angel the cat. His lifestyle actually. No school, lots of naps, up all night with lots of playtime. Not going to lie to you, house cats really know how to live . . .

~

I was watching a nature program about the life of a moth when my mother came into the room and stood near the couch, watching me. I felt awkward. I looked at her and smiled, then looked back at the TV. She asked me if I wanted a tomato sandwich. I shook my head. She asked me if I wanted to go for a walk. Or maybe get a snowball.

"Later maybe," I said. "Probably later."

"Okay," she said. I looked at her and she had this weak little smile on her face. I felt bad.

"No, really. I'd love to go for a walk, maybe a snowball . . . Or do anything with you, Mom. I really would. But right now I'm just, you know, really into this show about, um . . . moths. I've got to see what happens. But tomorrow we can, uh, go somewhere. I promise."

"Okay," she said. "Great."

I tried not to look at her. Dumb gray moths pounded themselves against a floodlight somewhere and I heard my mother sigh.

~

"Live life," says Mister Reese. "Take it for what it's worth and embrace it. Travel. Do things. Have fun and don't be scared. APPRECIATE life . . . And when you get old and nearly dead like me, don't look back and regret the things you didn't do. Because you won't be able to help regretting some of the things you did. And that's enough for anybody . . ."

~

Oh no. A few minutes ago I was smoking at the molehill with all my little mole friends when I saw from beneath the foliage, two pair of feet go past. One pair wore fuzzy slippers—definitely Mister Reese—but the other was wearing sneakers. Familiar sneakers. Donald Diamond–type sneakers. The same sneakers I'd shot with my pellet pistol just last month . . . I peered through the pine needles, squatting. There could be no mistake. Mister Reese and Donald Diamond were going for a walk. TOGETHER.

I thought about following them to see what they were up to. I almost did, but I was afraid Mister Reese would see me and think I was being weird. Jealous or something. So I wussed out.

~

Saw Donald today. He was sitting on the edge of the cul-de-sac, catching up on his summer reading. Something came over me when I saw him. Something always comes over me when I see him, but this time it was worse. A RAGE. It made me feel bad inside. I was jealous. He had been trying to steal my new friend just yesterday, possibly my only real friend, and I had caught him in the act, although he didn't know it yet. When he waved at me this morning with his goofy oversized hands, I couldn't take it. I began skipping stones at him, bouncing them across the pavement. I never even hit him, but he started crying anyway. He ran off and left his books behind in the mulch. I considered stomping them. But I didn't.

Instead I went over to Mister Reese's. I meant to confront him about Donald. If the two of them were going to be friends, then we most certainly could not be. But what had Donald told the old man about me? What poison had my enemy used? I wanted this info before I started doling out any ultimatums.

I didn't say anything at first. I tried to ease myself into the conversation . . .

Mister Reese and I smoked a little reefer and then we went out back so he could teach me a new song on the banjo. "The Old Home Place," it was called. I liked it very much, even though I had trouble learning it. I have trouble learning every song, but this one was different. It made me sad and happy at the same time. All I wanted was to be a little boy again, living at our old house on Charles Street. Before everything had gone to shit. I could do my whole life over again. Different though. I swear I could've cried if I wanted to. But I didn't.

I had to get myself together. I had come over here for a reason.

"So I heard you had a nice little walk with my old friend Donald yesterday?"

The old man showed no emotion one way or the other. He just let a stream of smoke spill from his lips and stared off into the trees. "Where did you hear that?" he asked.

"A little birdy told me," I said. "Actually it was a mole."

"Those moles seem pretty well informed considering the amount of time they spend in the dirt. But yes, Master Diamond approached me as I was taking a late afternoon stroll. Trying to jump-start the old circulatory system. Nice young fellow. We didn't travel very far together."

"Oh . . . So . . . What did you guys talk about?"

"You mostly."

"I knew it! What did he say!?"

"I gathered that he wanted to make friends with you. Or at least be cordial."

"*Friends!* Cordial! That's rich! What did he really say?"

"That was about it." Mister Reese adjusted himself in his chair. He picked a single sad string on the banjo before starting up again. "The kid just wanted to know why you hate him is all. I think he looks up to you. You're a little older than he is and he's still fresh from out of town. He's sure there must be something wrong with him if you don't like him. You should be nicer to Donald, if you want my advice. Life's too short to make enemies. You don't have to be blood brothers or anything. But you should at least treat him like you're both human. At least that's my take on the situation."

My heart sunk into my stomach and fell out my asshole. All the rage had left me and now I felt worse than before. Mister Reese was right as usual. What kind of person am I? I thought. What kind of person am I becoming? I excused myself with a lie about a French bread pizza I'd left in the oven and rushed back across the cul-de-sac, stoned as a martyr and emotional as hell, picking up Donald's books on the way.

I cleaned the books off and put them in an old Easter basket of mine that had been full of dirty lacrosse balls. I found some construction paper in my sisters' room and made a card that said "I'M SORRY" in big colorful block letters. On the inside I wrote, "For everything. My bad always, not yours. Friends, maybe? Or friendly?"

I left it on his doorstep and felt a lot better inside. Like I had just taken a huge shit. I wished my mother was at home so I could give her a hug.

~

"In this world of ours, Miles, there are only two ways to go about being rich," says Mister Reese. "Either work harder. Or need less." Then he pauses, smiling into the sun, and chuckles. "Marrying rich isn't a bad thing either. All things being equal. It worked all right for me. But I'll be dead and rotten before I admit doing it on purpose. Things just pan out that way sometimes. Magic, possibly. Or luck. Maybe both."

~

I came home to find my mom sitting in the dark. She was upset because she had to fly to Florida this week for work and she didn't want to go. Her voice sounded like a machine grinding rocks into gravel. It was a sad, tired voice.

The satellites and jet planes were starting to be visible in the sky. I know she likes to wish on them, so I asked her if she wanted to go for a walk and she said yes. We strolled around the community in circles. Little black birds or bats played in the sky overhead. We didn't really talk about anything in particular, but after a while we were holding hands. She was smiling. And I made wishes on just about every twinkling light my eyes could find.

~

I saw Donald Diamond this afternoon. He was hanging out near the high-voltage box with the rest of the little neighborhood goons. He waved hi to me! And I waved back!! Thumbs up even!!! I feel ABSOLVED!!!! Good, even great!!! I'm becoming a whole new person!!!!! MAYBE!!!!!!

~

My life is over. Late last night, I leave my mom's house to watch a *Star Wars* marathon on my dad's TV. I race over so I don't miss the "Long ago, in a galaxy far, far away . . ." opening line, which is so important to wrapping me up in the fantasy. I'm out of breath when I pull up to the back of the house. All the lights are on as I push my bike through the basement door. And what do I see before me but those identical little bitches sitting Indian-style on the carpet in front of MTV with you, dear Journal, spread open across their laps. They're giggling like a pair of lunatics, of course.

My sisters panic when they see me. I drop my bike and dive to snatch the composition book from their shitty claws. They're still cackling like they're under attack from the tickle monster, which pisses me off to no end. I don't want to tickle them but break their fingers instead. They squirm away from me and I try to get up but collapse on my chin, getting a rug burn in the process. Kelly yanks out a handful of crumpled pages and shoves them down her shirt before tossing the book at the floor in front of me. I stare at the cover a moment as the girls charge out of the room. I reach forward to see what pages they took. Mostly stuff about Ashley Vidal, I think. Maybe a few other things . . . When I complain to my father, he's busy on the Internet and my sisters have already gotten to him anyway, told him I was chasing them, so he just grunts at me and tells me to grow up, stop being so angry all the time.

I scoop up the journal and head back to my mother's. There's a hot breeze. I have a cigarette in my mouth. I shove the notebook behind my waistband as I ride. It sticks to the sweat on my belly. I make a conscious effort to take the long way home.

I pedal in jags, sprinting all fast and then coasting.

Pedal, pedal, coast . . . I wonder if keeping a journal is such a good idea. I consider burning you. Making you dead.

But then I put the thought from my head and decide to make up my mind about it later. My chances with Ashley are ruined, no matter what. Right?

Fuck a journal.

Fuck you, Journal.

You have no power over me.

~

I woke up this morning next to a big bowl of ice cream. It was melted and crawling with tiny ants. Hundreds of them. Thousands. Little black specks that wiggled around and lived off sugar. I was surprised Thomas Angel hadn't gotten them yet. They were lucky.

I had seen these animals around my mom's house more and more during these last few weeks of summer. One here, one there, maybe a small line or a cluster, but this was unprecedented. This was a regular insect rendezvous! All those little things, presumably with little brains that pulsed, congregating right here in my ice cream. A bowl of ice cream I didn't even remember eating last night. I sat on the edge of the couch and stared down into the bowl, weighing my options as I farted into the cushion.

Ants are small, but these guys were smaller than small, almost invisible. Their bodies were super delicate. I gently crushed one against the glass rim, then looked at the tip of my finger. He just disappeared. I had only been trying to pet him! Now he was gone. I looked deeper into the sludge at the bottom of the bowl.

Some of the ants were stuck in the ice cream. Kicking, thrashing. Maybe drowning even. Many others were walking on top of the mess, using the surface tension like Jesus on the Sea of Galilee or a kind of frog I saw the other day on the Discovery Channel. Some ants visited the depths of the bowl, while others milled about the walls or even balanced themselves on the rim like that poor little guy who disappeared in the last paragraph. All were eating.

I wondered if some ants were eating more ice cream than others. They were all so infinitesimally small. And there was more than enough melted French vanilla to go around. If each ant was eating a similar portion, then why risk venturing down into the deep and getting stuck, almost drowning? Maybe to make room for the other ants, I thought. I liked that thought. The more the merrier. The ant family was having a party.

Clearly these ants were harmless. In fact I sort of liked them. Even though they would undoubtedly fall into the category of pest if I had to categorize them. Besides, I didn't feel ready to leave the couch just yet. So I left the bowl on the coffee table and let the ants do their thing while I turned on the television.

We watched a show about water buffalo together before I decided I was ready for breakfast. I picked up the bowl of ants before heading into the kitchen. It was a good thing really, I told myself, to have so many ants together at once, in my bowl. I could really do some serious damage to the local population. Maybe even a final solution to the ant problem. That would be good for my mother.

I put the bowl in the sink and turned on the faucet. The ants tried to run away, scrambling in every direction, but they were already drowning, rushing down the drain with the flood.

Then I turned on the garbage disposal. I don't know why I did it because the ants were already done for and their little bodies were too fine to be totally chopped up by the blades. But I did it anyway. I turned on the blades.

~

I wake up beneath the weight of two adolescent girls and a cat. The cat stayed over at my dad's house last night while my mother was out of town. All three of them are jumping on my bed. Katie and Kelly are trying to kill me, I think. Thomas Angel is in on the plot. I put the pillow over my head and squeeze . . .

I'm still alive. The girls come in peace. Using my mattress and sleeping body as a trampoline is part of their apology. They're sorry for reading my journal.

"Even though it was funny," Kelly points out. They want me to walk with them to pick up some donuts. Their treat. I know I should still be angry, but I'm a real softy inside. I can't stay mad at anybody and I'm a sucker for anything free.

We're walking past the gatehouse, my sisters in little pink flip-flops and me in bare feet because I can't find my sneakers, and I start to ask them about the pages they tore out, whether they showed them to Ashley Vidal yet. But then I get embarrassed and shut my mouth. So I'm delighted when Katie volunteers some info. She tells me that Ashley actually thinks I'm kind of cute, although I'm a little old for her. But still, "kinda cute" is nice to hear.

"Ashley's even younger than WE are, Miles," Kelly chimes in, pointing back and forth between Katie and herself. "It's a little weird to be dating somebody younger than your little sisters. Especially when you're fourteen years old."

"I'm almost fifteen," I remind her.

"That might make it even weirder. I'm not sure. She's twelve."

I kick a stone out into the street with my bandaged toe and it stings. "Whatever," I sigh. Then, "It was just a little crush."

"Ashley and Retard, sitting in a tree," Kelly sings. "K-I-S-S-I-N-G."

"I'm sure she would think it was sweet," Katie says, putting her arm on my shoulder.

"WAIT." I pop out in front of them and stand there like a police blockade. "You didn't show her?"

"Not yet." Kelly grins at me like a cat. "But we can always hold it over your head."

"Like a giant piano."

"Thanks guys. It's wonderful to have you in my life. Wonderful sisters you are."

"We try," they say as a chorus, stopping to curtsey in unison.

The sun is already burning up the pavement and melting the garbage in the trash cans overflowing along York Road. The sun is in my eyes. The bottom of my foot nearly hits against the pancaked remains of a dead rat. I think a group of boys is following us on the other side of the street. But still, I'm feeling pretty swell. I'm glad to walk for donuts with my sisters.

The floor inside Dunkin' Donuts is dirtier than the sidewalk. I can feel the dust on my toes. It feels soft. We get one dozen assorted and a box of Munchkins. Coconut and jelly are my favorites. Katie pays the Indian fellow at the counter and we leave the store.

On our way out of the store, I notice the gang of boys still lurking on the other side of the street. Waiting for us. I turn away from them and guide my sisters past the Rite Aid and Corky's Liquors, where I used to get all my lame beer promos.

From behind me I hear someone call out, "Hey Blondie!" Which quickly turns into "Bitch! Gimme a donut!"

The girls are nervous and whisper to keep moving, walk faster, don't turn around, just ignore them. But I do turn around. Instinctively, I guess. Whatever. I turn.

It would be easy to describe them as a group of black boys, except that two of them are definitely white. Between the five boys, all about my age, there are two bikes being wheeled across the street in our direction—a BMX job with only one peg and a small girl's bike covered in Dora the Explorer decals. The boys are smiling like they'd just found a treasure chest left out on somebody's stoop.

I could feel the blood starting to heat up in my veins.

"Why you scared of us, shorty?" the second tallest boy asks me as they get a little closer. Apparently he is the leader. The twins are pulling at my arms, trying to get me to leave. There are plenty of people around, walking past us on the sidewalk, but no one seems to be doing anything. Can't anyone see the way these guys are looking at my sisters?

"Yo looks like a puppy dog with that spot on his face," one of the white boys hisses through a pair of thin lips and a slimy dirt-stache. "He be shitting himself like one too, yo."

Their whole crew is laughing at me.

"He look like Snoopy, yo."

Kelly is yelling at me to leave, run away, and Katie is starting to offer these guys our donuts if they will leave us alone and they probably would leave us alone but I'm not sure if I've even said anything to them yet, I'm just standing there with a tingling sensation racing up and down my skin, boiling inside. When one of the boys pushes me aside so he can get closer to my sisters and the donuts, black spots appear in my vision. I slam my fist into his temple. *CRACK.* I've definitely busted my fingers, I'm telling myself as a bike tire is jammed into my crotch. I fall forward and grab a chubby boy for support, but ultimately bring him down with me. I start clawing at him, trying to poke out his eyes. But I can't see anything. I'm shoving my fingers up his nose and into his cheeks, slamming his head into the pavement, all the while being pummeled on both sides and now in my head with a barrage of heel kicks and wild punches. There are chunks of donuts and blood and powdered sugar everywhere. People are crying. My sisters are crying and the chubby boy beneath me is crying and there is crying somewhere else, somewhere extremely close by, but I can't exactly tell where . . .

The last thing I think of as the boys smother me beneath their weight and a shitload of jabs to the face is that I would gladly sacrifice my body, my skin, my bones and cartilage for a good solid crack at someone's nose. I want to feel a nose break against my hand and hear it squish up into a brain, see the blood, feel it wet on my skin. Basically, I want to kill somebody. Anybody. But, as it is, I keep getting rocked by these punches . . .

My sisters have long run off when the old woman helps me up. She is old, but very large and has no problem lifting me up off the street. I am a little bit dazed. I lean against her fat tit for a second, probably getting her dress all gross and bloody in the process. She wants to take me to the hospital but I'm all right, I don't want to go, she can't make me, I live just down the street . . . I ask her about my sisters.

"The two tiny blonde white girls?"

"They're twins," I cough.

"I seen them take off into Homeland, sugar. Them boys you was fighting took off in the other direction."

"Thank you," I pant. I'm very out of breath.

"You sure you don't want to go to no hospital?"

I shake my head and spit a stream of blood out onto the sidewalk. One of my molars is cracked. A piece of it comes out in my spit. "I'm fine," I say, trying to restore my balance against the brick wall.

"Whatever you say, baby."

I nod and she walks away, shaking her head in disbelief. My sisters probably hate me right now, I think. I was only trying to help them. But I fuck everything up.

I'm about to limp off myself when something shiny and red catches my eye on the sidewalk. Something gleaming bright red in the heat, like a ruby. A bloodstone. I bend over to examine it. Half a jelly donut broken on the concrete and bleeding out its side.

I pick it up. It's soggy.
I put it in my mouth.
I stumble toward home.

~

After breaking into my mom's empty house and writing in my journal, I headed over to Mister Reese's place to get high and be comforted. I didn't want to see my sisters. I was feeling alone and I was all smashed up and bloody. I sat on the kitchen tiles and scribbled in my composition book, so the old man seemed like my only option.

Mister Reese was out on a walk when I got there, but Diamontay came to the door with Tickles and let me inside. Tickles the snake looked almost as bad as I felt. He was frozen solid around Diamontay's neck, just staring off into space like he was already dead.

"What happened to your body, little man?" Diamontay asked me over her shoulder, already hurrying off to unpack her first-aid gear. "I know those wounds didn't come off a skateboard."

She took Tickles upstairs. She led me to a stool in the kitchen. She was already dabbing peroxide on my knuckles where all the skin had come off. It stung like a motherfucker but I tried to not let on.

She made me pull my shirt over my head so she could see the bruises on my ribs.

"Somebody enjoyed theyself on this job," she said. "More like a few some*bodies* enjoyed you."

"I got in a fight with some Govans boys over on York Road. They were fucking with my little sisters, trying to steal our donuts."

"Your sisters are one thing, but you know you don't need to be fighting over something like donuts. Fuck a donut. Look at you now."

She held up a compact for me to see my face in. I was looking pretty rough. My face was all bruised and my lip was split open again, right where I had been stitched up earlier this summer. "For a donut. Now, don't you feel stupid?"

I nodded, looked down at my shoe.

Diamontay was shaking her head. She leaned in to smooth my hair and kiss me on the forehead, which was pretty scratched up but not nearly as bruised as the rest of my face. Her lips were big and soft and covered in Vaseline. I smiled at her and she smiled back. She patted me on the head again and whispered, "Don't you feel too bad, Miles. Everybody gets beat down one way or another sometime. It makes you a better person when you've had to survive a little abuse. Otherwise how would you know what to compare the good things to?"

"Thank you," I said. "For helping me. You and the old man are good friends to me."

"Good friends are the only friends you need, bud. A good friend is just about the best thing in the world a person can be," she said. "The old man is the best. But never tell him that."

"Thanks again," I said as she applied a Band-Aid to my cheekbone. "Sincerely."

And I really meant it. And I knew she could tell I meant it. And that was nice.

Then she kissed me on the forehead again.

That was nice too.

~

Secret: Sometimes I sit on the edge of my bed to get dressed so I can pretend I'm special for putting on my pants two legs at a time. I don't see myself continuing this practice any longer. I'm not sure why I wanted so bad to be special, but I don't think it was working.

~

Tickles the snake is very sick. He is suffering from paralysis and chronic regurgitation. Mister Reese and Diamontay are all messed up over it. I suggested the animal hospital where Robby works, but Diamontay already has a snake specialist out in western Maryland. I wish there was some way I could help . . . As it is, school is starting next week and I haven't even touched my reading list . . .

~

The Yankees came to town with all their stupid fans, so my father took off work and we went to the ball game. We were right behind the home team dugout and the O's were getting crushed.

My dad had been a little upset when he first saw the condition my face was in. He was sorry I would have to start out at a new school with a face full of cuts and bruises. I told him I didn't mind. He asked me if I was nervous about starting high school and I told him, "No." Then I changed my mind and said, "A little bit."

"You'll do fine," he said. He wrapped his big arm around my shoulder and squeezed me tight. He was hurting a deep purple bruise on my back, but I didn't want to let on. "I know you will," he said.

"Yeah," I said. "I guess so."

"Just remember, whatever doesn't kill you makes you stronger. And at your age, with so much going on and so much ahead of you, that whatever can work like steroids. Mark my words, you'll make it out alive. And stronger than an ox."

We hadn't spoken like this in a while. I started to thank him, but the Oriole bird got in the way, grabbing me by the brim of my hat and shaking his crotch in my face.

When the O-bird was finished with me, my father was laughing hysterically. He pointed up at the big screen, where my face was glowing enormous, grinning and beaten all to shit. The bird was pointing at me. I couldn't help but laugh.

~

The inside of the house is spotless and empty. The ghost shapes of the old furniture hiding beneath their oilcloth covers are missing. Every last personal knickknack has been packed up and moved into storage. The floor is shiny. Even the painters' things are gone. Outside, the house has been stripped bare as well. There are huge sacks of ivy sitting out by the trash. I'm on the roof outside my old window, smoking cigarettes and watching the clouds move across a patch of blue sky above me. They move slowly east, fluffy white giants plodding toward the sea. The world is huge. I feel tiny. I can feel the sun on my mashed-up face, inside the wounds. I hear a car pull into the driveway.

I climb up and stand by the chimney to get a better look at my visitor. A middle-aged woman with medium-length brown hair wrapped in a flowery shawl-thing. She hops out of her Kia and sits a wicker basket on the hood. She faces the house and takes a humongous breath into her lungs. Exhales. She holds her arms out toward the house, like she is going to give it a hug. I can't tell if she sees me or not. That air-hug might have been some form of greeting. Maybe she's a foreigner. So I step away from the chimney. I wave down to her as the cars zoom past on Charles.

And I scare the living shit out of her in the process.

I call to her. She shakes her head. I cup my hands over my mouth and try again. What is she, deaf? I scramble down off the broken slate roof, in through the window, downstairs, and out the front door to where the woman is standing in my front yard.

Turns out that she is. Deaf. For real deaf, but she reads lips so I soon get the story, albeit in a retarded kind of accent—which it turns out I find sort of pretty. The effort she puts into speaking, the dull sound at the edges of her voice . . . I find the whole thing charming. I've never met a deaf person before, I don't think. She is nice . . . her name is Melinda . . . I invite her inside.

She tells me she's one of the six children raised in the house before we lived there, four of whom were deaf. I already know the story of course. Her father had built the place all by himself with a construction crew consisting mostly of family. Having six deaf children in the house accounts for all the first floor bedrooms apparently, which we used to use as things like workout rooms or offices. See, Melinda's family had to live on the same floor to communicate since they couldn't hear each other. They couldn't shout upstairs like most families.

Melinda says she saw the house in *The Baltimore Sun*'s real estate listings while looking for a place of her own. She is a newlywed. I wonder if her husband is also deaf, but I decide not to ask.

The ad brought back memories, she tells me in her weird but nice voice. Before she knew it she had grabbed her basket in a fit of nostalgia and hopped in her car to make the drive all the way from Kingsville. She was on a mission to see the old house and collect a basketful of the brainy green Osage oranges to use as a centerpiece for her dining room table, just like her mom used to do when she was a little girl. It really is a beautiful story, especially in that pretty deaf voice.

We take a tour of the house and she shows me all these landmarks from her family's life: where her brother split his head open on the corner of a table, where her father and mother renewed their vows on their golden anniversary, where the kids used to measure themselves against the wall, where she got her period for chrissakes . . . For a deaf woman this lady sure can talk! And fast too! She's like a radio commercial, but I don't mind. It's cool learning about the past life of a place I always called home.

It's weird though.

Even though I was aware of the former tenants, I had always sort've seen this place as being my own.

And now it wasn't like that anymore.

It was just a place.

It belonged to the people who lived there, whenever they did.

"So why is your family selling?" Melinda asks me on our way outside to gather the pus-filled fruits.

"Div . . . orce," I say with an exaggerated shrug.

I can't think of a lie. Why bother?

"I'm sorry," she tells me.

"It is okay," I tell her. I've been enunciating super carefully to make sure she can read my lips. "You can . . . not . . . stay in . . . one place . . . for . . . ev . . . er . . . I . . . sup . . . pose." But Melinda is bent over sifting through these stinky old fruits and she can't even see my lips to read them. I feel stupid. "No one can quit moving forward without crashing, or stopping at least," I say to the birds and the trees.

"Oooooooh!" Melinda gasps, turns to face me. Her grin gets wide and she reaches out to me with both hands. She is cupping a mammoth Osage orange the color of glowing ooze. "Look!" she chirps, dead serious in her beautiful little retarded voice. "I found a good one!"

And for no reason at all we both start giggling like baffled infants and everything in the world feels safe for a second and I try to make that second last, but the next one comes instead.

~

Tickles the snake has been put to rest. It turns out he was suffering from something called Inclusion Body Disease, which has apparently grown increasingly common among certain species of domestic pythons and boas. The disease was rendering him blind and paralyzed. His nervous system was covered in lesions and he was suffering from something called "mouth-rot." Atrophy was taking over his spleen. He was going to die soon anyway. At least that's what the vet told us. He allowed us to bury Tickles ourselves, in the far corner of a pet cemetery near Gaithersburg.

Diamontay tried to hold back her tears when the doctor told her, but I could tell she was just being tough. Mister Reese held her hand in the waiting room. I didn't know what to do, I wasn't sure what purpose I could serve, but I felt like I was supposed to be there. I wanted to be a good friend to these people because they had been good to me this summer. Tickles, too.

The hole was about the size of a human's grave, only narrower. Behind it there was a dogwood tree and a patch of black-eyed Susans. There was a layer of clouds between us and the sun. It lit the scene like a black-and-white movie. The three of us stood together in a clump, holding the snake in a long, thin canvas bag shaped like one of those long cold cuts they serve at parties. We stood silent, looking down into the grave. I saw tiny worms playing in the dirt.

The three of us said a silent prayer and Diamontay started crying. Mister Reese held her tight against his tiny chest and started to get a little choked up himself. I was starting to feel it too, but I didn't want to think about death. I tried to imagine all the little worms and insects living in the dirt below us. Probably moles too, I thought, somewhere around here. Animals and dirt and then more dirt and rocks and then more rocks all the way down to a pit of molten rock and fire. And here I was living out my life on top of all that stuff, like a fly crawling across the skin of a melon. It seemed so . . . *unlikely*. Ridiculous too. It felt like all of life, everything we did, was only because we didn't know what else to do. And now a snake had died and we were burying him in the ground. I reached over and squeezed Diamontay's arm. I could tell she needed it.

We each dropped a shovelful of dirt on the body. Mister Reese and I crossed ourselves, but Diamontay only wrung her hands and cried. I don't think Diamontay is Catholic. After the snake was buried, I picked three black-eyed Susans and we put them on top of the mound. The tombstone, a little bronze plaque, was being ordered and would be there next week. But Diamontay wasn't sure that she would come back to see it. "Gotta keep on keepin' on," she said, trying not to cry. "The only direction we can move is forward. Water off a duck's back, right? And I'm a duck. Let's all be ducks."

On the way home, we tried not to talk about Tickles. Change the subject. Mister Reese asked me if I was nervous about starting school. I told him I was still worried about writing my personal essay. I mean, what on earth do I know about anything, particularly myself? How could I possibly teach anyone else about my life, which I had so much trouble understanding? Much less keep them interested. Of course, Mister Reese had an answer.

"Listen, anyone can be interesting to almost anyone else at any time, Miles. Everyone. Even boring people with boring lives. Every single body has something going on inside it. It all depends on what parts you choose to reveal."

I told him I guessed he was right.

"He is," Diamontay whispered in a sad little voice. "Pretty smart for a dummy . . ."

She broke out laughing as tears rolled down her face and we laughed along with her and the car felt better inside, buzzing almost, and I think we each felt a little better inside for a while too.

But on the other hand, high school starts next week and my personal essay is due. Despite all of Mister Reese's good advice and everything else that has happened this summer, I can't figure out why anyone in their right mind should want to read fifteen hundred words about me.

ACKNOWLEDGMENTS

The author would like to thank his friends, family, Madison Smartt Bell, Carabella Sands, Mississippi John Hurt, as well as all of the wonderful neighborhoods and communities here in Baltimore, past and present, that have informed this book.

Author photograph © Tim Ford

ABOUT THE AUTHOR

TIMMY REED is a writer, teacher, and native of Baltimore, Maryland. He received his M.F.A. from the University of Baltimore. Reed is the author of the books *IRL*, *Miraculous Fauna*, and *The Ghosts That Surrounded Them*. His short fiction has been featured in the *Wigleaf* Top 50 on multiple occasions and has appeared in *Necessary Fiction* and the *Atticus Review*, among other publications. In 2015, he won the Baker Artist Awards Semmes G. Walsh Award. He teaches English at Stevenson University and Community College of Baltimore County and English as a Second Language at Morgan State University.